Memento Mori

by MURIEL SPARK
available from New Directions:

THE ABBESS OF CREWE

ALL THE POEMS OF MURIEL SPARK

ALL THE STORIES OF MURIEL SPARK

THE BACHELORS

THE BALLAD OF PECKHAM RYE

THE COMFORTERS

THE DRIVER'S SEAT

A FAR CRY FROM KENSINGTON

THE GHOST STORIES

THE GIRLS OF SLENDER MEANS

LOITERING WITH INTENT

MEMENTO MORI

OPEN TO THE PUBLIC

THE PUBLIC IMAGE

ROBINSON

SYMPOSIUM

Muriel Spark

MEMENTO MORI

A NEW DIRECTIONS CLASSIC

Manufactured in the United States of America
New Directions Books are printed on acid-free paper.
First published as a New Directions Classic in 2000
Published by arrangement with Dame Muriel Spark, and her agent Georges Borchardt, Inc., New York.

Library of Congress Cataloging in Publication Data
Spark, Muriel.
    Memento Mori / Muriel Spark.
        p. cm. — (New Directions classics)
    ISBN 978-0-8112-1438-4 (alk.paper)
        1. Aged--England--London--Fiction. 2. Aged—Psychology--Fiction. 3. Practical jokes—Fiction. 4. London (England)—Fiction. I. Title. II. Series.

PR6037.P29 M4 2000
823'.914—dc21

                                99-058767

New Directions Books are published for James Laughlin
by New Directions Publishing Corporation,
80 Eighth Avenue, New York 10011

FIFTH PRINTING

Memento Mori

What shall I do with this absurdity—
O heart, O troubled heart—this caricature,
Decrepit age that has been tied to me
As to a dog's tail?

—W. B. YEATS, *The Tower*

O what venerable and reverent creatures did
the aged seem! Immortal Cherubims!

—THOMAS TRAHERNE,
Centuries of Meditation

Q. What are the four last things to be ever
    remembered?
A. The four last things to be ever remem-
    bered are Death, Judgment, Hell, and
    Heaven.

—*The Penny Catechism*

Chapter One

Dame Lettie Colston refilled her fountain pen and continued her letter:

One of these days I hope you will write as brilliantly on a happier theme. In these days of cold war I *do* feel we should soar above the murk & smog & get into the clear crystal.

The telephone rang. She lifted the receiver. As she had feared the man spoke before she could say a word. When he had spoken the familiar sentence she said, "Who is that speaking, who is it?"

But the voice, as on eight previous occasions, had rung off.

Dame Lettie telephoned to the Assistant Inspector as she had been requested to do. "It has occurred again," she said.

"I see. Did you notice the time?"

"It was only a moment ago."

"The same thing?"

"Yes," she said, "the same. Surely you have some means of tracing—"

"Yes, Dame Lettie, we will get him, of course."

A few moments later Dame Lettie telephoned to her brother Godfrey.

"Godfrey, it has happened again."

"I'll come and fetch you, Lettie," he said. "You must spend the night with us."

"Nonsense. There is no danger. It is merely a disturbance."

"What did he say?"

"The same thing. And quite matter-of-fact, not really threatening. Of course the man's mad. I don't know what the police are thinking of, they must be sleeping. It's been going on for six weeks now."

"Just those words?"

"Just the same words—'*Remember you must die*'—nothing more."

"He must be a maniac," said Godfrey.

Godfrey's wife, Charmian, sat with her eyes closed, attempting to put her thoughts into alphabetical order which Godfrey had told her was better than no order at all, since she now had grasp of neither logic nor chronology. Charmian was eighty-five. The other day a journalist from a weekly paper had been to see her. Godfrey had subsequently read aloud to her the young man's article:

> . . . By the fire sat a frail old lady, a lady who once set the whole of the literary world (if not the Thames) on fire. . . . Despite her age, this legendary figure is still abundantly alive. . . .

Charmian felt herself dropping off, and so she said to the maid, who was arranging the magazines on the long oak table by the window, "Taylor, I am dropping off to sleep for five minutes. Telephone to St. Mark's and say I am coming."

Just at that moment Godfrey entered the room holding his hat and wearing his outdoor coat. "What's that you say?" he said.

"Oh, Godfrey, you made me start."

"*Taylor* . . ." he repeated, "St. Mark's . . . Don't you realise there is no maid in this room, and furthermore, you are not in Venice."

"Come and get warm by the fire," she said, "and take your coat off"; for she thought he had just come in from the street.

"I am about to go *out,*" he said. "I am going to fetch Lettie who is to stop with us to-night. She has been troubled by another of those anonymous calls."

"That was a pleasant young man who called the other day," said Charmian.

"Which young man?"

"From the paper. The one who wrote—"

"That was five years and two months ago," said Godfrey.

"Why can't one be kind to her?" he asked himself as he drove to Lettie's house in Hampstead. "Why can't one be more gentle?" He himself was eighty-seven, and in charge of all his faculties. Whenever he considered his own behaviour he thought of himself not as "I" but as "one."

"One has one's difficulties with Charmian," he told himself.

"Nonsense," said Lettie. "I have no enemies."

"*Think,*" said Godfrey. "Think hard."

"The red lights," said Lettie. "And don't talk to me as if I were Charmian."

"Lettie, if you please, I do not need to be told how to drive. I observed the lights." He had braked hard, and Dame Lettie was jerked forward.

She gave a meaningful sigh which, when the green lights came on, made him drive all the faster.

"You know, Godfrey," she said, "you are wonderful for your age."

"So everyone says." His driving pace became moderate;

her sigh of relief was inaudible, her patting herself on the back invisible.

"In your position," he said, "you must have enemies."

"Nonsense."

"I say *yes*." He accelerated.

"Well, perhaps you're right." He slowed down again, but Dame Lettie thought, I wish I hadn't come.

They were at Knightsbridge. It was only a matter of keeping him happy till they reached Kensington Church Street and turned into Vicarage Gardens where Godfrey and Charmian lived.

"I have written to Eric," she said, "about his book. Of course, he has something of his mother's former brilliance, but it did seem to me that the subject-matter lacked the joy and hope which was the mark of a good novel in those days."

"I couldn't *read* the book," said Godfrey. "I simply could not go on with it. A motor salesman in Leeds and his wife spending a night in a hotel with that communist librarian . . . Where does it all lead you?"

Eric was his son. Eric was fifty-six and had recently published his second novel.

"He'll never do as well as Charmian did," Godfrey said. "Try as he may."

"Well, I can't quite agree with that," said Lettie, seeing that they had now pulled up in front of the house. "Eric has a hard streak of realism which Charmian never—"

Godfrey had got out and slammed the door. Dame Lettie sighed and followed him into the house, wishing she hadn't come.

"Did you have a nice evening at the pictures, Taylor?" said Charmian.

"I am not Taylor," said Dame Lettie, "and in any case, you always called Taylor Jean during her last twenty or so years in your service."

Mrs. Anthony, their daily housekeeper, brought in the milky coffee and placed it on the breakfast table.

"Did you have a nice evening at the pictures, Taylor?" Charmian asked her.

"Yes, thanks, Mrs. Colston," said the housekeeper.

"Mrs. Anthony is not Taylor," said Lettie. "There is no one by name of Taylor here. And anyway you used to call her Jean latterly. It was only when you were a girl that you called Taylor Taylor. And, in any event, Mrs. Anthony is not Taylor."

Godfrey came in. He kissed Charmian. She said, "Good morning, Eric."

"He is not Eric," said Dame Lettie.

Godfrey frowned at his sister. Her resemblance to himself irritated him. He opened *The Times*.

"Are there lots of obituaries to-day?" said Charmian.

"Oh, don't be gruesome," said Lettie.

"Would you like me to read you the obituaries, dear?" Godfrey said, turning the pages to find the place in defiance of his sister.

"Well, I should like the war news," Charmian said.

"The war has been over since nineteen forty-five," Dame Lettie said. "If indeed it is the last war you are referring to. Perhaps, however, you mean the First World War? The Crimean perhaps . . . ?"

"Lettie, please," said Godfrey. He noticed that Lettie's hand was unsteady as she raised her cup, and the twitch on her large left cheek was pronounced. He thought in how much better form he himself was than his sister, though she was the younger, only seventy-nine.

Mrs. Anthony looked round the door. "Someone on the phone for Dame Lettie."

"Oh, who is it?"

"Wouldn't give a name."

"Ask who it is, please."

"Did ask. Wouldn't give—"

"I'll go," said Godfrey.

Dame Lettie followed him to the telephone and overheard the male voice. "Tell Dame Lettie," it said, "to remember she must die."

"Who's there?" said Godfrey. But the man had hung up.

"We must have been followed," said Lettie. "I told no one I was coming over here last night."

She telephoned to report the occurrence to the Assistant Inspector.

He said, "Sure you didn't mention to anyone that you intended to stay at your brother's home?"

"Of course I'm sure."

"Your brother actually heard the voice? Heard it himself?"

"Yes, as I say, he took the call."

She told Godfrey, "I'm glad you took the call. It corroborates my story. I have just realised that the police have been doubting it."

"Doubting your word?"

"Well, I suppose they thought I might have imagined it. Now, perhaps, they will be more active."

Charmian said, "The police . . . What are you saying about the police? Have we been robbed?"

"I am being molested," said Dame Lettie.

Mrs. Anthony came in to clear the table.

"Ah, Taylor, how old are you?" said Charmian.

"Sixty-nine, Mrs. Colston," said Mrs. Anthony.

"When will you be seventy?"

"Twenty-eighth November."

"That will be splendid, Taylor. You will then be one of us," said Charmian.

Chapter Two

There were twelve occupants of the Maud Long Medical Ward (aged people, female). The ward sister called them the Baker's Dozen, not knowing that this is thirteen, but having only heard the phrase; and thus it is that a good many old sayings lose their force.

First came a Mrs. Emeline Roberts, seventy-six, who had been a cashier at the Odeon in the days when it *was* the Odeon. Next came Miss or Mrs. Lydia Reewes-Duncan, seventy-eight, whose past career was uncertain, but who was visited fortnightly by a middle-aged niece, very bossy towards the doctors and staff, very uppish. After that came Miss Jean Taylor, eighty-two, who had been a companion-maid to the famous authoress Charmian Piper after her marriage into the Colston Brewery family. Next again lay Miss Jessie Barnacle who had no birth certificate but was put down as eighty-one, and who for forty-eight years had been a newsvendor at Holborn Circus. There was also a Madame Trotsky, a Mrs. Fanny Green, a Miss Doreen Valvona, and five others, all of known and various careers, and of ages ranging from seventy to ninety-three. These twelve old women were known variously as Granny Roberts, Granny Duncan, Granny Taylor, Grannies Barnacle, Trotsky, Green, Valvona, and so on.

Sometimes, on first being received into her bed, the patient would be shocked and feel rather let down by being called Granny. Miss or Mrs. Reewes-Duncan threatened for a whole week to report anyone who called her Granny Duncan. She threatened to cut them out of her will and to write to her M.P. The nurses provided writing-paper and a pencil at her urgent request. However, she changed her mind about informing her M.P. when they promised not to call her Granny any more. "But," she said, "you shall never go back into my will."

"In the name of God that's real awful of you," said the ward sister as she bustled about. "I thought you was going to leave us all a packet."

"Not now," said Granny Duncan. "Not now, I won't. You don't catch me for a fool."

Tough Granny Barnacle, she who had sold the evening paper for forty-eight years at Holborn Circus, and who always said, "Actions speak louder than words," would send out to Woolworth's for a will-form about once a week; this would occupy her for two or three days. She would ask the nurse how to spell words like "hundred" and "ermine."

"Goin' to leave me a hundred quid, Granny?" said the nurse. "Goin' to leave me your ermine cape?"

The doctor on his rounds would say, "Well, Granny Barnacle, am I to be remembered or not?"

"You're down for a thousand, Doc."

"My word, I must stick in with you, Granny. I'll bet you've got a long stocking, my girl."

Miss Jean Taylor mused upon her condition and upon old age in general. Why do some people lose their memories, some their hearing? Why do some talk of their youth and others of their wills? She thought of Dame Lettie Colston who had all her senses intact, and yet played a real will-game, attempting to keep the two nephews in suspense, enemies of each other. And Charmian . . . Poor Charmian, since her stroke. How muddled she was about most things, and yet perfectly sensible when she discussed the books she had written. Quite clear on just that one thing, the subject of her books.

A year ago, when Miss Taylor had been admitted to the ward, she had suffered misery when addressed as Granny Taylor, and she thought she would rather die in a ditch than be kept alive under such conditions. But she was a woman practised in restraint; she never displayed her resentment. The lacerating familiarity of the nurses' treatment merged in with her arthritis, and she bore them both as long as she could without complaint. Then she was forced to cry out with pain during a long haunted night when the dim ward lamp made the beds into grey-white lumps like terrible bundles of laundry which muttered and snored occasionally. A nurse brought her an injection.

"You'll be better now, Granny Taylor."

"Thank you, nurse."

"Turn over, Granny, that's a good girl."

"Very well, nurse."

The arthritic pain subsided, leaving the pain of desolate humiliation, so that she wished rather to endure the physical nagging again.

After the first year she resolved to make her suffering a voluntary affair. If this is God's will then it is mine. She gained from this state of mind a decided and visible dignity, at the same time as she lost her stoical resistance to pain. She complained more, called often for the bed pan, and did not hesitate, on one occasion when the nurse was dilatory, to wet the bed as the other grannies did so frequently.

Miss Taylor spent much time considering her position. The doctor's "Well, how's Granny Taylor this morning? Have *you* been making your last will and test—" would falter when he saw her eyes, the intelligence. She could not help hating these visits, and the nurses giving her a hair-do, telling her she looked like sixteen, but she volunteered mentally for them, as it were, regarding them as the Will of God. She reflected that everything could be worse, and was sorry for the youngest generation now being born into the world, who in their old age, whether of good family or no, educated or no, would be forced by law into Chronic Wards; she dared say every citizen in the Kingdom would take it for granted; and the time would surely come for everyone to be a government granny or grandpa, unless they were mercifully laid to rest in their prime.

Miss Doreen Valvona was a good reader, she had the best eyes in the ward. Each morning at eleven she read aloud everyone's horoscope from the newspaper, holding it close to her brown nose and, behind her glasses, to the black eyes which came from her Italian father. She knew by heart everyone's Zodiacal sign. "Granny Green—Virgo," she would say. " 'A day for bold measures. Close partnerships are beneficial. A wonderful period for entertaining.' "

"Read us it again. My hearing aid wasn't fixed."

"No, you'll have to wait. Granny Duncan's next. Granny Duncan—Scorpio. 'Go all out for what you want to-day. Plenty of variety and gaiety to keep you on your toes.' "

Granny Valvona remembered everyone's horoscope all the day, checking up to see the points where it came true, so that, after Dame Lettie Colston had been to visit Granny Taylor, the old family servant, a cry arose from Granny Valvona: "What did I tell you in your horoscope? Listen while I read it out again. Granny Taylor—Gemini. 'You are in wonderful form to-day. Exceptionally bright social potents are indicated.' "

" 'Portents,' " said Miss Taylor. "Not potents."

Granny Valvona looked again. She spelt it out. "Potents," she said. Miss Taylor gave it up, murmuring, "I see."

"Well?" said Granny Valvona. "Wasn't that a remarkable forecast? 'You are in wonderful form to-day. Exceptionally bright social' . . . Now isn't that your visitor foretold, Granny Taylor?"

"Yes indeed, Granny Valvona."

"Some dame!" said the littlest nurse, who could not make out why Granny Taylor had so seriously called her visitor "Dame Lettie." She had heard of dames as jokes, and at the pictures.

"Wait, nurse, I'll read your horoscope. What's your month?"

"I've to go, Granny Valvoni. Sister's on the hunt."

"Don't call my name Valvoni, it's Valvona. It ends with an *ah*."

"*Ah*," said the little nurse, and disappeared with a hop and a skip.

"Taylor was in wonderful form to-day," Dame Lettie told her brother.

"You've been to see Taylor? You are really very good," said Godfrey. "But you look tired, I hope you haven't tired yourself."

"Indeed, I felt I could have changed places with Taylor. Those people are so fortunate these days. Central heating, everything they want, plenty of company."

"Is she in with nice people?"

"Who—Taylor? Well they all look splendid and clean. Taylor always says she is perfectly satisfied with everything. So she should be."

"Got all her faculties still?" Godfrey was obsessed by the question of old people and their faculties.

"Certainly. She asked for you and Charmian. She cries a little of course at the mention of Charmian. Of course she was fond of Charmian."

Godfrey looked at her closely. "You look ill, Lettie."

"Utter nonsense. I'm in wonderful form to-day. I've never felt more fit in my life."

"I don't think you should return to Hampstead," he said.

"After tea. I've arranged to go home after tea, and after tea I'm going."

"There was a telephone call for you," said Godfrey.

"Who was it?"

"That chap again."

"Really? Have you rung the C.I.D.?"

"Yes. In fact, they're coming round to-night to have a talk with us. They are rather puzzled about some aspects of the case."

"What did the man say? What did he say?"

"Lettie, don't upset yourself. You know very well what he said."

"I go back to Hampstead after tea," said Lettie.

"But the C.I.D.—"

"Tell them I have returned to Hampstead."

Charmian came unsteadily in. "Ah, Taylor, have you enjoyed your walk? You look in wonderful form to-day."

"Mrs. Anthony is late with tea," said Dame Lettie, moving her chair so that her back was turned to Charmian.

"You must not sleep alone at Hampstead," said Godfrey. "Call on Lisa Brooke and ask her to stop with you for a few days. The police will soon get the man."

"Lisa Brooke be damned," said Dame Lettie, which would have been an alarming statement if intended seriously, for Lisa Brooke was not many moments dead, as Godfrey discovered in *The Times* obituary the next morning.

Chapter Three

Lisa Brooke died in her seventy-third year, after her second stroke. She had taken nine months to die, and in fact it was only a year before her death that, feeling rather ill, she had decided to reform her life, and reminding herself how attractive she still was, offered up the new idea, her celibacy, to the Lord to whom no gift whatsoever is unacceptable.

It did not occur to Godfrey as he marched into a pew in the crematorium chapel that anyone else present had ever been Lisa's lover except himself. It did not even come to mind that he had been Lisa's lover, for he had never been her lover in any part of England, only Spain and Belgium, and at the moment he was busy with statistics. There were sixteen people present. On first analysis it emerged that five were relatives of Lisa. Next, among the remaining eleven, Godfrey elicited Lisa's lawyer, her housekeeper, the bank manager. Lettie had just arrived. Then there was himself. That left six, only one of whom he recognised, but all of whom were presumably Lisa's hangers-on, and he was glad their fountain of ready cash had dried up. All those years of daylight robbery; and many a time he had told Lisa, "A child of six could do better than that," when she displayed one of the paintings, outrages committed by one of her pets. "If he hasn't made his way in the world by now," he had said, time and again, of old Percy Mannering the poet, "he never will. You are a fool, Lisa, letting him drink your gin and shout his poetry in your ears."

Percy Mannering, almost eighty, stood with his lean stoop as the coffin was borne up the aisle. Godfrey stared hard at the poet's red-veined hatchet cheekbones and thin nose. He thought, I bet he's regretting the termination of his income. They've all bled poor Lisa white. . . . The poet was, in fact, in a state of excitement. Lisa's death had filled him with thrilling awe, for though he knew the general axiom that death was everyone's lot he could never realise the particular case; each new death gave him something fresh to feel. It came to him as the service began that within a few minutes Lisa's coffin would start sliding down into the furnace, and he saw as in a fiery vision her flame-tinted hair aglow as always, competing with the angry tresses of the fire below. He grinned like an elated wolf and shed tears of human grief as if he were half-beast, half-man, instead of half-poet, half-man. Godfrey watched him and thought, He must be senile. He has probably lost his faculties.

The coffin began to slide slowly down the slope towards a gap in the wall while the organ played something soft and religious. Godfrey, who was not a believer, was profoundly touched by this ensemble, and decided once and for all to be cremated when his time came. "There goes Lisa Brooke," he said to himself as he saw the last tilt of the coffin. The prow, thought the poet, lifts, and the ship goes under with the skipper on board. . . . No, that's too banal, Lisa herself as the ship is a better idea. Godfrey looked round him and thought, She should have been good for another ten years, but what can you expect with all that drink and all these spongers? So furiously did he glare about him that he startled the faces which caught his eye.

Tubby Dame Lettie caught up with her brother in the aisle as he moved with the others to the porch. "What's the matter with you, Godfrey?" Lettie breathed.

The chaplain was shaking doleful hands with everyone at the door. As Godfrey gave his hand he said over his shoulder to Lettie, "The matter with *me?* What d'you mean what's the matter with me? What's the matter with *you?*"

Lettie, as she dabbed her eyes, whispered, "Don't talk so loud. Don't glare so. Everyone's looking at you."

On the floor of the long porch was a muster of flowers done up, some in tasteful bunches, one or two in old-fashioned wreaths. These were being inspected by Lisa's relatives, her middle-aged nephew and his wife, her parched elder sister Janet Sidebottome who had been a missionary in India at a time when it *was* India, her brother Ronald Sidebottome who had long since retired from the City and Ronald's Australian wife who had been christened Tempest. Godfrey did not immediately identify them, for he saw only the row of their several behinds as they stooped to examine the cards attached to each tribute.

"Look, Ronald, isn't this sweet? A tiny bunch of violets —oh, see, it says, 'Thank you, Lisa dear, for all those wonderful times, with love from Tony.' "

"Rather odd words. Are you sure—"

"Who's Tony, I wonder?"

"See, Janet, this huge yellow rose wreath here from Mrs. Pettigrew. It must have cost her a fortune."

"What did you say?" said Janet who did not hear well.

"A wreath from Mrs. Pettigrew. It must have cost a fortune."

"Sh-sh-sh," said Janet, looking round. True enough, Mrs. Pettigrew, Lisa's old housekeeper, was approaching in her well-dressed confident manner. Janet, cramped from the card-inspection, straightened painfully and turned to meet Mrs. Pettigrew. She let the woman grip her hand.

"Thank you for all you have done for my sister," said Janet sternly.

"It was a pleasure." Mrs. Pettigrew spoke in a surprisingly soft voice. It was understood Janet was thinking of the will. "I loved Mrs. Brooke, poor soul."

Janet inclined her head graciously, firmly withdrew her hand and rudely turned her back.

"Can we see the ashes?" loudly enquired Percy Mannering as he emerged from the chapel. "Is there any hope of *seeing* them?" At the noise he made, Lisa's nephew and wife jumped nervily and looked round.

"I want to see those ashes if possible." The poet had cornered Dame Lettie, pressing his hungry demand. Lettie felt there was something unhealthy about the man. She moved away.

"That's one of Lisa's artists," she whispered to John Sidebottome, not meaning to prompt him to say "Oh!" and lift his hat in Percy's direction, as he did.

Godfrey stepped backwards and stood on a spray of pink carnations. "Oh—sorry," he said to the carnations, stepping off them quickly, and then was vexed at his folly, and knew that in any case no one had seen him after all. He ambled away from the trampled flowers.

"What's that fellow want with the ashes?" he said to Lettie.

"He wants to see them. Wants to see if they've gone grey. He is quite disgusting."

"Of course they will be grey. The fellow must have lost his faculties. *If* he ever had any."

"I don't know about faculties," said Lettie. "Certainly he has no feelings."

Tempest Sidebottome, blue-haired and well corseted was saying in a voice which carried away out to the Garden of Remembrance: "To some people there's just nothing that's sacred."

"Madam," said Percy, baring his sparse green teeth in a smile, "the ashes of Lisa Brooke will always be sacred to me. I desire to see them, kiss them if they are cool enough. Where's that cleric? He'll have the ashes."

"Do you see over there—Lisa's housekeeper?" Lettie said to Godfrey.

"Yes, yes, I wonder—"

"That's what *I'm* wondering," said Lettie, who was wondering if Mrs. Pettigrew wanted a job, and if so would agree to undertake the personal care of Charmian.

"But I think we would need a younger woman. That one must be getting on," said Godfrey, "if I remember aright."

"Mrs. Pettigrew has a constitution like a horse," said Dame Lettie, casting a horse-dealer's glance over Mrs. Pettigrew's upright form. "And it is impossible to get younger women."

"Has she got all her faculties?"

"Of course. She had poor Lisa right under her thumb."

"I hardly think Charmian would want—"

"Charmian needs to be bullied. What Charmian needs is a firm hand. She will simply go to pieces if you don't keep at her. Charmian needs a firm hand. It's the only way."

"But what about Mrs. Anthony?" said Godfrey. "The woman might not get on with Mrs. Anthony. It would be tragic if we lost her."

"If you don't find someone soon to look after Charmian you will certainly lose Mrs. Anthony. Charmian is too much of a handful for Mrs. Anthony. You will lose Mrs. Anthony. Charmian keeps calling her Taylor. She is bound to resent it. Who are you staring at?"

Godfrey was staring at a short bent man walking with the aid of two sticks round a corner of the chapel. "Who is that man?" said Godfrey. "He looks familiar."

Tempest Sidebottome fussed over to the little man who beamed up at her with a fresh face under his wide black hat. He spoke in a shrill boyish tone. "Afraid I'm late," he said. "Is the party over? Are you all Lisa's sinisters and bothers?"

"That's Guy Leet," said Godfrey, at once recognising him, for Guy had always used to call sisters and brothers sinisters and bothers. "The little rotter," said Godfrey, "he used to be after Charmian. It must be thirty-odd years since last I saw him. He can't be more than seventy-five and just see what he's come to."

Tables at a tea-shop near Golders Green had been reserved for Lisa's post-crematorial party. Godfrey had intended to miss the tea party but the arrival of Guy Leet had changed his mind. He was magnetized by the sight of the clever little man doubled over his sticks, and could not keep his eyes off the arthritic hobbling of Guy making his way among the funeral flowers.

"Better join them for tea," he said to Lettie, "hadn't we?"

"What for?" said Lettie, looking round the company. "We can have tea at home. Come back with me for tea, we can have it at home."

"I think we'd better join them," said Godfrey. "We might have a word with Mrs. Pettigrew about her taking on Charmian."

Lettie saw Godfrey's gaze following the hunched figure of Guy Leet who, on his sticks, had now reached the door of his taxi. Several of the party helped Guy inside, then joined him. As they drove off, Godfrey said, "Little rotter. Supposed to be a critic. Tried to take liberties with all the lady novelists, and then he was a theatre critic and he was after the actresses. You'll remember him, I daresay."

"Vaguely," said Lettie. "He never got much change out of *me*."

"He was never after you," said Godfrey.

At the tea-shop Dame Lettie and Godfrey found the

mourners being organised into their places by Tempest
Sidebottome, big and firm in her corsets, aged seventy-five,
with that accumulated energy which strikes despair in the
hearts of jaded youth, and which now fairly intimidated
even the two comparative youngsters in the group, Lisa's
nephew and his wife who were not long past fifty.

"Ronald, sit down here and stay put," Tempest said
to her husband, who put on his glasses and sat down.

Godfrey was casting about for Guy Leet, but in the
course of doing so his sight was waylaid by the tables on
which were set silver-plate cakestands with thin bread and
butter on the bottom tier, cut fruitcake above that, and
on the top, a pile of iced cakes wrapped in cellophane
paper. Godfrey began to feel a passionate longing for his
tea, and he pushed past Dame Lettie to stand conspicu-
ously near the organiser, Tempest. She did notice him
right away and allotted him a seat at a table. "Lettie," he
called then, "come over here. We're sitting here."

"Dame Lettie," said Tempest over his head, "you must
come and sit with us, my dear. Over here beside Ronald."

Damned snob, thought Godfrey. I suppose she thinks
Lettie is somebody.

Someone leant over to offer him a cigarette which was
a filter-tip. However, he said, "Thanks, I'll keep it for
after tea." Then looking up, he saw the wolf grin on the
face of the man who was offering him the packet with a
trembling hand. Godfrey plucked out a cigarette and
placed it beside his plate. He was angry at being put beside Percy Mannering, not only because Percy had been
one of Lisa's spongers, but also because he must surely be
senile with that grin and frightful teeth, and Godfrey felt
the poet would not be able to manage his teacup with
those shaking hands.

He was right, for Percy spilled a lot of his tea on the
cloth. He ought to be in a home, thought Godfrey. Tempest glanced at their table every now and then and tut-

tutted a lot, but she did this all round, as if it were a children's beanfeast. Percy was oblivious of the mess he was making or of anyone's disapproval. Two others sat at their table, Janet Sidebottome and Mrs. Pettigrew. The poet had taken it for granted that he was the most distinguished and therefore the leader of conversation.

"One time I fell out with Lisa," he roared, "was when she took up Dylan Thomas." He pronounced the first name Dye-lan. "Dylan Thomas," he said, "and Lisa was good to him. Do you know, if I was to go to Heaven and find Dylan Thomas there, I'd prefer to go to HELL. *And* I wouldn't be surprised if Lisa hasn't gone to Hell for aiding and abetting him in his poetry, so-called."

Janet Sidebottome bent her ear closer to Percy. "What did you say about poor Lisa? I don't hear well."

"I say," he said, "I wonder if Lisa's gone to Hell because of her—"

"From respect to my dear sister," said Janet, with a hostile look, "I don't think we will discuss—"

"Dye-lan Thomas died from D.T." said the old poet, becoming gleeful. "You see the coincidence? His initials were D. T. and he *died* from D.T. Hah!"

"In respect for my late sister—"

"Poetry!" said Percy. "Dylan Thomas didn't know the meaning of the word. As I said to Lisa, I said, 'You're, making a bloody fool of yourself supporting that charlatan. It isn't poetry, it's a leg-pull.' She didn't see it, nobody saw it, but I'm telling you his verse was all a HOAX."

Tempest turned round in her chair. "Hush, Mr. Mannering." she said, tapping Percy on the shoulder.

Percy looked at her and roared, "Ha! Do you know what you can tell Satan to do with Dye-lan Thomas's poetry?" He sat back to observe, with his two-fanged gloat, the effect of this question, which he next answered in unprintable terms, causing Mrs. Pettigrew to say, "Gracious!" and to wipe the corners of her mouth with her handkerchief. Meanwhile various commotions arose at the other tables and the senior waitress said, "Not in *here,* sir!"

Godfrey's disgust was arrested by fear that the party might now break up. While everyone's attention was still on Percy he hastily took a couple of the cellophane-wrapped cakes from the top tier of the cakestand, and stuffed them into his pocket. He looked round and felt sure no one had noticed the action.

Janet Sidebottome leaned over to Mrs. Pettigrew. "What did he say?" she said.

"Well, Miss Sidebottome," said Mrs. Pettigrew, meanwhile glancing at herself sideways in a glass on the wall, "as far as I could comprehend, he was talking about some gentleman indelicately."

"Poor Lisa," said Janet. Tears came to her eyes. She kissed her relatives and departed. Lisa's nephew and his wife sidled away, though before they had reached the door they were summoned back by Tempest because the nephew had left his scarf. Eventually, the couple were permitted to go. Percy Mannering remained grinning in his seat.

To Godfrey's relief Mrs. Pettigrew refilled his cup. She also poured one for herself, but when Percy passed his shaking cup she ignored it. Percy said, "Hah! That was strong meat for you ladies, wasn't it?" He reached for the teapot. "I hope it wasn't me made Lisa's sister cry," he said solemnly. "I'd be sorry to have made her cry." The teapot was too heavy for his quivering fingers and fell from them on to its side, while a leafy brown sea spread from the open lid over the tablecloth and on to Godfrey's trousers.

Tempest rose, pushing back her chair as if she meant business. She was followed to the calamitous table by Dame Lettie and a waitress. While Godfrey was being sponged, Lettie took the poet by the arm and said, "Please go." Tempest, busy with Godfrey's trousers, called over her shoulder to her husband, "Ronald, you're a man. Give Dame Lettie a hand."

"What? Who?" said Ronald.

"Wake up, Ronald. Can't you see what has to be done? Help Dame Lettie to take Mr. Mannering outside."

"Oh," said Ronald, "why, someone's spilt their tea!" He ogled the swimming tablecloth.

Percy shook off Dame Lettie's hand from his arm and, grinning to right and left, buttoning up his thin coat, departed.

A place was made for Godfrey and Mrs. Pettigrew at the Sidebottomes' table. "Now we shall have a fresh pot of tea," said Tempest. Everyone gave deep sighs. The waitresses cleaned up the mess. The room was noticeably quiet.

Dame Lettie started to question Mrs. Pettigrew about her future plans. Godfrey was anxious to overhear this conversation. He was not sure that he wanted Lisa Brooke's housekeeper to look after Charmian. She might be too old or too expensive. She looked a smart woman, she might have expensive ideas. And he was not sure that Charmian would not have to go into a home.

"There's no definite offer, of course," he interposed.

"Well, Mr. Colston, as I was saying," said Mrs. Pettigrew, "I can't make any plans, myself, until things are settled."

"What things?" said Godfrey.

"Godfrey, please," said Lettie, "Mrs. Pettigrew and I are having a chat." She slumped her elbow on the table and turned to Mrs. Pettigrew, cutting off her brother from view.

"What is your feeling about the service?" said Tempest.

Godfrey looked round at the waitresses. "Very satisfactory," he said. "That older one handled that Mannering very well, I thought."

Tempest closed her eyes as one who prays for grace. "I mean," she said, "poor Lisa's rites at the crematorium."

"Oh," said Godfrey, "you should have said funeral service. When you said the service, naturally I thought—"

"What do you feel about the cremation service?"

"First rate," said Godfrey. "I've quite decided to be cremated when my time comes. Cleanest way. Dead bodies under the ground only contaminate our water supplies. You should have said cremation service in the first place."

"I thought it was cold," said Tempest. "I do wish the minister had read out poor Lisa's obituary. The last cremation I was at—that was Ronald's poor brother Henry—they read out his obituary from the *Nottingham Guardian,* all about his war service and his work for SSAFA and Road Safety. It was so very moving. Now why couldn't they have read out Lisa's? All that in the papers about what she did for the Arts, he should have read it out to us."

"I quite agree," said Godfrey. "It was the least he could have done. Did you make a special request for it?"

"No," she sighed. "I left the arrangements to Ronald. Unless you do everything yourself . . ."

"They always get very violent about other poets," said Ronald. "You see, they feel very personal about poetry."

"Whatever is he talking about?" said Tempest. "He's talking about Mr. Mannering, that's what he's on about. We aren't talking about Mr. Mannering, Ronald. Mr. Mannering's left, it's a thing of the past. We've gone on to something else."

As they rose to leave Godfrey felt a touch on his arm. Turning round he saw Guy Leet behind him, his body crouched over his sticks and his baby face raised askew to Godfrey's.

"Got your funeral-baked meats all right?" said Guy.

"What?" said Godfrey.

Guy nodded his head towards Godfrey's pocket which bulged with the cakes. "Taking them home to Charmian?"

"Yes," said Godfrey.

"And how is Charmian?"

Godfrey had partly regained his poise. "She's in wonderful form," he said. "I'm sorry," he said, "to see you having such a difficult time. Must be terrible not being able to get about on your own pins."

Guy gave a high laugh. He came close to Godfrey and breathed into his waistcoat, "But I *did* get about, dear fellow. At least I did."

On the way home Godfrey threw the cakes out of his car window. Why did one pocket those damned things? he thought. One doesn't need them, one could buy up every cake-shop in London and never miss the money. Why did one do it? It doesn't make sense.

"I have been to Lisa Brooke's funeral," he said to Charmian when he got home, "or rather, cremation."

Charmian remembered Lisa Brooke; she had cause to remember her. "Personally, I'm afraid," said Charmian, "that Lisa was a little spiteful to me sometimes, but she had her better side. A generous nature when dealing with the right person, but—"

"Guy Leet was there," said Godfrey. "He's nearly finished now, bent over two sticks."

Charmian said, "Oh, and what a clever man he was!"

"Clever?" said Godfrey.

Charmian, when she saw Godfrey's face, giggled squeakily through her nose.

"I have quite decided to be cremated when my time comes," said Godfrey. "It is the cleanest way. The cemeteries only pollute our water supplies. Cremation is best."

"I do so agree with you," said Charmian sleepily.

"No, you do *not* agree with me," he said. "R.C.'s are not allowed to be cremated."

"I mean, I'm sure you are right, Eric dear."

"I am not Eric," said Godfrey. "You are not sure I'm right. Ask Mrs. Anthony, she'll tell you that R.C.'s are against cremation." He opened the door and bawled for Mrs. Anthony. She came in with a sigh.

"Mrs. Anthony, you're a Roman Catholic, aren't you?" said Godfrey.

"That's right. I've got something on the stove."

"Do you believe in cremation?"

"Well," she said, "I don't really much like the idea of being shoved away quick like that. I feel somehow it's sort of—"

"It isn't a matter of how you feel, it's a question of what your Church says you've not got to do. Your Church says you must not be cremated, that's the point."

"Well, as I say, Mr. Colston, I don't really fancy the idea—"

" 'Fancy the idea' . . . It is not a question of what you fancy. You have no choice in the matter, do you see?"

"Well, I always like to see a proper burial, I always like—"

"It's a point of discipline in your Church," he said, "that you mustn't be cremated. You women don't know your own system."

"I see, Mr. Colston. I've got something on the stove."

"*I* believe in cremation, but you don't—Charmian, you disap*prove* of cremation, you understand."

"Very well, Godfrey."

"And you too, Mrs. Anthony."

"O.K., Mr. Colston."

"On principle," said Godfrey.

"That's right," said Mrs. Anthony and disappeared.

Godfrey poured himself a stout whisky and soda. He took from a drawer a box of matches and a razor blade and set to work, carefully splitting the slim length of each match, so that from one box of matches he would eventually make two boxfuls. And while he worked he sipped his drink with satisfaction.

Chapter Four

The reason Lisa Brooke's family arranged her post-funeral party at a tea-shop rather than at her small brick studio-house at Hampstead was this. Mrs. Pettigrew, her housekeeper, was still in residence there. The family had meanwhile discovered that Lisa had bequeathed most of her fortune to Mrs. Pettigrew whom they had long conceived as an unfortunate element in Lisa's life. They held this idea in the way that people often are obscurely right, though the suspicions that lead up to their conclusions are faulty. Whatever they suspected was the form that Mrs. Pettigrew's influence over Lisa took, they hoped to contest Lisa's will if possible, on the grounds that Lisa, when she made it, was not in her right mind, and probably under undue influence of Mrs. Pettigrew.

The very form of the will, they argued, proved that Lisa had been unbalanced when she made it. The will had not been drafted by a lawyer. It was a mere sheet of writing paper, witnessed by the charwoman and her daughter a year before Lisa's death, bequeathing her entire fortune "to my husband if he survives me, and thereafter to my housekeeper, Mabel Pettigrew." Now Lisa, so her relatives believed, had no husband alive. Old Brooke was long dead, and moreover Lisa had been divorced from him during the Great War. She must have been dotty, they argued, even to mention a husband. The sheet of paper, they insisted, must be invalid. Alarmingly, their lawyers saw nothing invalid on the face of it; Mrs. Pettigrew was apparently the sole beneficiary.

Tempest Sidebottome was furious. "Ronald and Janet," she said, "should inherit by rights. We'll fight it. Lisa would never have mentioned a husband had she been in her right mind. Mrs. Pettigrew must have had a hold on Lisa."

"Lisa was always liable to say foolish things," Ronald Sidebottome remarked.

"You're a born obstructionist," Tempest said.

Hence, they had felt it cautious to avoid the threshold of Harmony Studio for the time being, and had felt it equally cautious to invite Mrs. Pettigrew to the tea-shop.

Dame Lettie was explaining this to Miss Taylor, who had seen much in her long service with Charmian. Dame Lettie had, unawares, in the past few months, slipped into the habit of confiding in Miss Taylor. So many of Lettie's contemporaries, those who knew her world and its past, had lost their memories or their lives, or were away in private homes in the country; it was handy having Miss Taylor available in London to discuss things with.

"You see, Taylor," said Dame Lettie, "they never did like Mrs. Pettigrew. Now, Mrs. Pettigrew is an admirable woman. I was hoping to persuade her to take on Charmian. But of course with Lisa's money in prospect, she does not intend to work any longer. She must be over seventy, although of course she says . . . Well, you see, with Lisa's money—"

"She would never do for Charmian," said Miss Taylor.

"Oh really, I feel Charmian needs a firm hand if we are to keep her at home. Otherwise she will have to go into a nursing home. Taylor, you have no conception how irritated poor Godfrey gets. He tries his best." Dame Lettie lowered her voice. "And then, Taylor, there is the lavatory question. Mrs. Anthony can't be expected to take her every time. As it is, Godfrey attends to the chamber pots in the morning. He isn't used to it, Taylor, he's not used to that sort of thing."

In view of the warm September afternoon Miss Taylor had been put out on the balcony of the Maud Long Ward where she sat with a blanket round her knees.

"Poor Charmian," she said, "darling Charmian. As we get older these affairs of the bladder and kidneys do become so important to us. I hope she has a commode by her bedside, you know how difficult it is for old bones to manage a pot."

"She has a commode," said Dame Lettie. "But that doesn't solve the daytime problem. Now Mrs. Pettigrew would have been admirable in that respect. Think what she did for poor Lisa after the first stroke. However, Mrs. Pettigrew is out of the question because of this inheritance from Lisa. It was ridiculous of Lisa."

Miss Taylor looked distressed. "It would be tragic," she said, "for Mrs. Pettigrew to go to the Colstons'. Charmian would be most unhappy with the woman. You must not think of such a thing Dame Lettie. You don't know Mrs. Pettigrew as I do."

Dame Lettie's yellow-brown eyes focused as upon an exciting scene as she bent close to Miss Taylor. "Do you think," she enquired, "there was anything peculiar, I mean not right, between Mrs. Pettigrew and Lisa Brooke?"

Miss Taylor did not pretend not to know what she meant. "I cannot say," she said, "what were the habits of their relationship in former years. I only know this, and you yourself know, Dame Lettie, Mrs. Pettigrew was very domineering towards Mrs. Brooke in the last eight or nine years. She is not suitable for Charmian."

"It is precisely because she is domineering," said Lettie, "that I wanted her for Charmian. Charmian *needs* a bully. For her own good. But anyway, that's beside the point, Mrs. Pettigrew does not desire the job. I understand Lisa has left her practically everything. Now Lisa was very comfortable as you know, and—"

"I would not be sure that Mrs. Pettigrew will in fact inherit," insisted Miss Taylor.

"No, Taylor," said Dame Lettie, "I'm afraid Lisa's family do not stand a chance. I doubt if their advisers will let them take it to court. There is no case. Lisa was perfectly sane to the day she died. It is true Mrs. Pettigrew had an undesirable influence over Lisa, but Lisa was in her right mind to the end."

"Yes, it is true Mrs. Pettigrew had a hold on her."

"I wouldn't say a hold, I would say an influence. If Lisa was fool enough—"

"Quite, Dame Lettie. Was Mr. Leet at the funeral, by any chance?"

"Oh, Guy Leet was there. I shouldn't think he will last long. Rheumatoid arthritis with complications." Dame Lettie recalled, as she spoke, that rheumatoid arthritis was one of Miss Taylor's afflictions, but, she thought, after all she must face the facts. "Very advanced case," said Dame Lettie, "he was managing with great difficulty on two sticks."

"It is like wartime," Miss Taylor remarked.

"What do you say?"

"Being over seventy is like being engaged in a war. All our friends are going or gone and we survive amongst the dead and the dying as on a battlefield."

She is wandering in her mind and becoming morbid, thought Dame Lettie.

"Or suffering from war nerves," said Miss Taylor.

Dame Lettie was annoyed, because she had intended to gain some advice from Miss Taylor.

"Come now, Taylor," she said. "You are talking like Charmian."

"I must," said Miss Taylor, "have caught a lot of her ways of thought and speech."

"Taylor," said Lettie, "I want to ask your advice." She looked at the other woman to see if she was alert. "Four months ago," she said, "I began to receive anonymous telephone calls from a man. I have been receiving them ever since. On one occasion when I was staying with Godfrey, the man, who must have traced me there, gave a message for me to Godfrey."

"What does he say?" said Miss Taylor.

Dame Lettie leant to Miss Taylor's ear and, in a low tone, informed her.

"Have you told the police?"

"Of course we have told the police. They are useless. Godfrey had an interview with them too. Useless. They seem to think we are making it up."

"You will have thought of consulting Chief Inspector Mortimer who was such a fan of Charmian's?"

"Of course I have not consulted Mortimer. Mortimer is retired, he is close on seventy. Time passes, you know. You are living in the past, Taylor."

"I only thought," said Miss Taylor, "that Inspector Mortimer might act privately. He might at least be helpful in some way. He always struck me as a most unusual—"

"Mortimer is out of the question. We want a young, active detective on this job. There is a dangerous lunatic at large. I know not how many people besides myself are endangered."

"I should not answer the telephone, Dame Lettie, if I were you."

"My dear Taylor, one can't be cut off perpetually. I still have my Homes to consider, I am not entirely a back number, Taylor. One must be on the phone. But I confess, I am feeling the strain. Imagine for yourself every time one answers the telephone. I never know if one is going to hear that distressing sentence. It *is* distressing."

" 'Remember you must die,' " said Miss Taylor.

"Hush," said Dame Lettie, looking warily over her shoulder.

"Can you not ignore it, Dame Lettie?"

"No, I cannot. I have tried, but it troubles me deeply. It *is* a troublesome remark."

"Perhaps you might obey it," said Miss Taylor.

"What's that you say?"

"You might, perhaps, try to remember you must die."

She is wandering again, thought Lettie. "Taylor," she said, "I do not wish to be advised how to think. What I hoped you could suggest is some way of apprehending the criminal, for I see that I must take matters into my own hands. Do you understand telephone wires? Can you follow the system of calls made from private telephone boxes?"

"It's difficult," said Miss Taylor, "for people of advanced years to start remembering they must die. It is best to form the habit while young. I shall think of some plan, Dame Lettie, for tracing the man. I did once know something about the telephone system, I will try to recall what I knew."

"I must go." Lettie rose, and added, "I expect you are keeping pretty well, Taylor?"

"We have a new ward sister here," said Miss Taylor. "She is not so pleasant as the last. I have no complaint personally, but some of my companions are inclined to be touchy, to imagine things."

Lettie cast her eye along the sunny verandah of the Maud Long Ward where a row of old women sat out in their chairs.

"They are fortunate," said Dame Lettie and uttered a sigh.

"I know it," said Miss Taylor. "But they are discontented and afraid."

"Afraid of what?"

"The sister in charge," said Miss Taylor.

"But what's wrong with her?"

"Nothing," said Miss Taylor, "except that she is afraid of these old people."

"*She* is afraid? I thought you said the patients were afraid of *her*."

"It comes to the same thing," said Miss Taylor.

She is wandering, thought Lettie, and she said, "In the Balkan countries, the peasants turn their aged parents out of doors every summer to beg their keep for the winter."

"Indeed?" said Miss Taylor. "That is an interesting system." Her hand, when Dame Lettie lifted it to say goodbye, was painful at the distorted joints.

"I hope," said Miss Taylor, "you will think no more of employing Mrs. Pettigrew."

Dame Lettie thought, She is jealous of anyone else's having to do with Charmian.

Perhaps I am, thought Miss Taylor who could read Dame Lettie's idea.

And as usual after Dame Lettie had left, she pondered and understood more and more why Lettie came so frequently to visit her and seemed to find it pleasant, and at the same time seldom spoke or behaved pleasantly. It was the old enmity about Miss Taylor's love affair in 1907 which in fact Dame Lettie had forgotten—had dangerously forgotten; so that she retained in her mind a vague fascinating enmity for Jean Taylor without any salutary definition. Whereas Miss Taylor herself, until quite recently, had remembered the details of her love affair, and Dame Lettie's subsequent engagement to marry the man, which came to nothing after all. But recently, thought Miss Taylor, I am beginning to feel as she does. Enmity is catching. Miss Taylor closed her eyes and laid her hands loosely on the rug which covered her knees. Soon the nurses would come in to put the grannies to bed. Meanwhile she thought with a sleepy pleasure, I enjoy Dame Lettie's visits, I look forward to them, in spite of which

I treat her with my asperity. Perhaps it is because I have now so little to lose. Perhaps it is because these encounters have an exhilarating quality. I might sink into a torpor were it not for fat old Lettie. And perhaps, into the bargain, I might use her in the matter of the ward sister, although that is unlikely.

"Granny Taylor—Gemini. 'Evening festivities may give you all the excitement you want. A brisk day for business enterprises,' " Granny Valvona read out for the second time that day.

"There," said Miss Taylor.

The Maud Long Ward had been put to bed and was now awaiting supper.

"It comes near the mark," said Miss Valvona. "You can always know by your horoscope when your visitors are coming to see you, Granny Taylor. Either your Dame or that gentleman that comes; you can always tell by the stars."

Granny Trotsky lifted her wizened head with low brow and pug nose, and said something. Her health had been degenerating for some weeks. It was no longer possible to hear exactly what she said. Miss Taylor was the quickest in the ward at guessing what Granny Trotsky's remarks might be, but Miss Barnacle was the most inventive.

Granny Trotsky repeated her words, whatever they were.

Miss Taylor replied, "All right, Granny."

"What did she say?" demanded Granny Valvona.

"I am not sure," said Miss Taylor.

Mrs. Reewes-Duncan who claimed to have lived in a bungalow in former days, addressed Miss Valvona. "Are you aware that the horoscope you have just read out to us specifies evening festivities, whereas Granny Taylor's visitor came at three-fifteen this afternoon?"

Granny Trotsky again raised her curiously shaped head

and spoke, emphasising her statement with vehement nods of this head which was so fearfully and wonderfully made. Whereupon Granny Barnacle ventured, "She says festivities my backside. What's the use of the stars foretell with that murderous bitch of a sister outside there, she says, waiting to finish off the whole ward in the winter when the lot goes down with pneumonia. You'll be reading your stars, she says all right when they need the beds for the next lot. That's what she says—don't you, Granny Trotsky?"

Granny Trotsky, raising her head, made one more, and very voluble effort, then drooped exhausted on her pillow, closing her eyes.

"That's what she said," said Granny Barnacle. "And right she is, too. Come the winter them that's made nuisances of theirselves don't last long under that sort."

A ripple of murmurs ran up the rows of beds. It ceased as a nurse walked through the ward, and started again when she had gone.

Miss Valvona's strong eyes stared through her spectacles into the past, as they frequently did in the autumn, and she saw the shop door open on a Sunday afternoon, and the perfect ices her father manufactured, and heard the beautiful bellow of his accordion after night had fallen, on and on till closing time. "Oh, the parlour and the sundaes and white ladies we used to serve," she said, "and my father with the Box. The white ladies stiff on your plate, they were hard, and made from the best-quality products. And the fellows who would say to me, 'How do, Doreen,' even if they had another girl with them after the pictures. And my father got down the Box and played like a champion. It cost him fifty pounds, in those days, mind you it was a lot."

Granny Duncan addressed Miss Taylor, "Did you ask that Dame to do something for us, at all?"

"Not exactly," said Miss Taylor, "but I mentioned that

we were not so comfortable now as we have been previously."

"She goin' to *do* something for us?" demanded Granny Barnacle.

"She is not herself on the management committee," Miss Taylor explained. "It is a friend of hers who is on the committee. Now, it will take time. I can't, you know, press her. She is very easily put off. And then, you know, in the meantime, we must try to make the best of this." The nurse walked back through the ward among the grannies, all sullen and silent but for Granny Trotsky who had now fallen noisily asleep with her mouth open.

It was true, thought Miss Taylor, that the young nurses were less jolly since Sister Burstead had taken over the ward. Of course it was but two seconds before she had become "Sister Bastard" on the lips of Granny Barnacle. The associations of her name, perhaps, in addition to her age—Sister Burstead was well over fifty—had affected Granny Barnacle with immediate hostile feelings. "Over fifty they got the workhouse mind. You can't never trust a ward sister over fifty. They don't study that there's new ways of goin' on since the war, by law." These sentiments in turn had affected the other occupants of the ward. But the ground had been prepared the week before by their knowledge of the departure of the younger sister: "A change, hear that?—there's to be a change. What's the stars say, Granny Valvona?" Then, on the morning that Sister Burstead took over, she being wiry, bespectacled and middle-aged with a bad-tempered twitch at one side of her face between lip and jaw, Granny Barnacle declared she had absolutely placed her. "The workhouse mind. You see what'll happen now. Anyone that's a nuisance or can't contain themselves like me with Bright's disease, they won't last long in this ward. You get pneumonia in the winter, can't help but do, and that's her chance."

"What you think she'll do, Granny Barnacle?"

"Do? It's what she won't do. You wait to the winter, you'll be lyin' there and nothin' done for you. Specially if you got no relations or that to raise enquiries."

"The other nurses is all right, Granny, though."

"You'll see a difference in *them*."

There had been a difference. The nurses were terrified of their new superior, that was all. But as they became more brisk and efficient so did the majority of the grannies behold them with hostile thoughts and deadly suspicions. When the night staff came on duty the ward relaxed, and this took the form of much shouting throughout the night. The grannies shouted in their sleep and half-waking rest-lessness. They accepted their sedative pills fearfully, and in the morning would ask each other, "Was I all right last night?" not quite remembering whether they or another had made the noise.

"It all goes down in the book," said Granny Barnacle. "Nothing happens during the night but what it goes into the book. And Sister Bastard sees it in the morning. You know what that'll mean, don't you, when the winter comes?"

At first, Miss Taylor took a frivolous view of these say-ings. It was true the new sister was jittery and strict, and over fifty years of age, and frightened. It will all blow over, thought Miss Taylor, when both sides get used to the change. She was sorry for Sister Burstead and her fifty-odd years. Thirty years ago, thought Miss Taylor, I was into my fifties, and getting old. How nerve-racking it is to be getting old, how much better to be old! It had been touch and go, in those days, whether she would leave the Colstons and settle down with her brother in Coventry while she had the chance. It was such a temptation to leave them, she having been cultivated by twenty-five years' association with Charmian. By the time she was fifty it really seemed absurd for her to continue her service with Charmian, her habits and tastes were so superior to those of the maids she met on her travels with Charmian, she was so much more intelligent. She had been all on edge for the first two years of her fifties, not knowing whether to go to look after the widowed brother in Coventry and enjoy some status or whether to continue waking Charmian up every morning, and observing in silence Godfrey's infidelities. For two years while she made up her mind she had given Charmian hell, threatening to leave every month, folding Charmian's dresses in the trunk so that they were horribly creased, going off to art galleries while Charmian rang for her in vain.

"You're far worse now," Charmian would tell her, "than when you were going through the menopause."

Charmian plied her with bottles of tonic medicine which she had poured down the lavatory with a weird joy. At last, after a month's holiday with her brother in Coventry, she found she could never stand life with him and his ways, the getting him off to his office in the morning, the keeping him in clean shirts, and the avaricious whist parties in the evening. At the Colstons' there was always some exotic company, and Charmian's sitting-room had been done out in black and orange. All the time she was at Coventry Miss Taylor had missed the exciting scraps of conversation which she had been used to hearing on Charmian's afternoons.

"Charmian darling, don't you think, honestly, I should have Boris bumped off?"

"No, I rather like Boris."

And those telephone messages far into the nights.

"Is that you, Taylor darling? Get Charmian to the phone, will you? Tell her I'm in a state. Tell her I want to read her my new poem." That was thirty years ago.

Ten years before that, the telephone messages had been different again, "Taylor, tell Mrs. Colston I'm in London. Guy Leet. Not a word, Taylor to *Mr.* Colston." These were messages which Miss Taylor sometimes did not deliver. Charmian herself was going through her difficult age at that time, and was apt to fly like a cat at any man who made approaches to her, even Guy who had previously been her lover.

At the age of fifty-three Miss Taylor had settled down. She could even meet Alec Warner without any of the old feelings. She went everywhere with Charmian, sat for hours while Charmian read aloud her books, while still in manuscript, gave judgment. As gradually the other servants became difficult and left, so Jean Taylor took charge. When Charmian had her hair bobbed, so did Miss Taylor. When Charmian entered the Catholic Church Miss Taylor was received, really just to please Charmian.

She rarely saw her brother from Coventry, and when she did, counted herself lucky to have escaped him. On one occasion she told Godfrey Colston to watch his step. The disappointed twitch at the side of her mouth which had appeared during her forties, now gradually disappeared.

So it will be, thought Miss Taylor, in the case of Sister Burstead, once she settles down. The twitch will go.

Presently, however, Miss Taylor began to feel there was very little chance of the new sister's twitch disappearing. The grannies were so worked up about her, it would not be surprising if she did indeed let them die of pneumonia should she ever get the chance.

"You must speak to the doctor, Granny Barnacle," said Miss Taylor, "if you really feel you aren't getting the right treatment."

"The doctor my backside. They're hand-in-glove. What's a old woman to them? I ask you."

The only good that could be discerned in the arrival of the new sister was the fact that the ward was now more alert. Everyone's wits had improved, as if the sister were a sort of shock treatment. The grannies had forgotten their will-making, and no longer threatened to disinherit each other or the nurses.

Mrs. Reewes-Duncan, however, made the great mistake of threatening the sister with her solicitor one dinner-time when the meat was tough or off, Miss Taylor could not recall which. "Fetch the ward sister to me," Mrs. Reewes-Duncan demanded. "Fetch her here to me."

The sister marched in purposefully when thus summoned.

"Well, Granny Duncan, what's the matter? Hurry up now, I'm busy. What's the matter?"

"This meat, my good woman . . ." The ward felt at once that Granny Duncan was making a great mistake. "My niece will be informed. . . . My solicitor—"

For some reason, the word "solicitor" set fire to Sister Burstead. That one word did the trick. You could evidently threaten the doctor, the matron, or your relations, and she would merely stand there glaring angrily with her twitch, she would say no more than, "You people don't know you're born," and, "Fire ahead, tell your niece, *my dear.*" But the word solicitor fairly turned her, as Granny Barnacle recounted next day, arse over tit. She gripped the bedrail and yelled at Granny Duncan for a long time, it might have been ten minutes. Words, in isolation and grouped in phrases, detached themselves like sparks from the fiery scream proceeding from Sister Burstead's mouth. "Old beast . . . dirty old beast . . . food . . . grumble and grouse . . . I've been on since eight o'clock this morning . . . I've been on and on . . . work, work, work, day after day, for a lot of useless old, filthy old . . ."

Sister Burstead went off duty immediately assisted by a nurse. If only, thought Miss Taylor, we could try to be sweet old ladies, she would be all right. It's because we aren't sweet old things. . . .

"Scorpio," Granny Valvona had declared four hours later, although like everyone else in the ward she was shaken-up. "Granny Duncan—Scorpio. 'You can sail ahead with confidence. The success of another person could affect you closely.' " Granny Valvona put down the paper. "You see what I mean?" she said. "The stars never let you down. 'The success of another person . . .' A remarkable forecast."

The incident was reported to the matron and the doctor. The former made enquiries next morning of a kind which clearly indicated she was hoping against hope Sister Burstead could be exonerated, for she would be difficult to replace.

The matron bent over Miss Taylor and spoke quietly and exclusively. "Sister Burstead is having a rest for a few days. She has been overworking."

"Evidently," said Miss Taylor, whose head ached horribly.

"Tell me what you know of the affair. Sister Burstead was provoked, I believe?"

"Evidently," said Miss Taylor, eyeing the bland face above her and desiring it to withdraw.

"Sister Burstead was cross with Granny Duncan?" said the matron.

"She was nothing," said Miss Taylor, "if not cross. I suggest the sister might be transferred to another ward where there are younger people and the work is lighter."

"All the work in this hospital," said the matron, "is heavy."

Most of the grannies felt too upset to enjoy the few days' absence from duty of Sister Burstead, for whenever the general hysteria showed signs of waning, Granny Barnacle applied the bellows: "Wait till the winter. When you get pneumonia . . ."

During those days it happened that Granny Trotsky had her second stroke. An aged male cousin was summoned to her bedside, and a screen was put round her bed. He emerged after an hour still wearing the greenish-black hat in which he had arrived, shaking his head and hat, and crying all over his blotchy foreign face.

Granny Barnacle, who was up in her chair that day, called to him, "Pssst!"

Obediently he came to her side.

Granny Barnacle flicked her head towards the screened-in bed.

"She gone?"

"Nah. She breathe, but not speak."

"D'you know who done it?" said Granny Barnacle. "It was the sister that brought it on."

"She have no sister. I am next of kin."

A nurse came and hurried him away.

Granny Barnacle declared once more to the ward, "Sister Bastard done for Granny Trotsky."

"Ah but Granny, it was her second stroke. There's always a second, you know."

"Sister done it with her bad temper."

On learning that Sister Burstead had neither been dismissed nor transferred to another ward but was to return on the following day, Granny Barnacle gave notice to the doctor that she refused further treatment, was discharging herself next day, and that she would tell the world why.

"I know my bloody rights as a patient," she said. "Don't think I don't know the law. *And* what's more, I can get the phone number of the newspaper. I only got to ring up and they come along and want to know what's what."

"Take it easy, Granny," said the doctor.

"If Sister Bastard comes back, I go," said Granny Barnacle.

"Where to?" said the nurse.

Granny Barnacle glared. She felt that the nurse was being sarcastic, must know that she had spent three months in Holloway prison thirty-six years ago, six months twenty-two years ago, and subsequently various months. Granny Barnacle felt the nurse was referring to her record when she said "Where to?" in that voice of hers.

The doctor frowned at the nurse and said to Granny

Barnacle, "Take it easy, Granny. Your blood pressure isn't too good this morning. What sort of a night did you have? Pretty restless?"

This speech unnerved Granny Barnacle who had indeed had a bad night.

Granny Trotsky, who had so far recovered that the bed-screen had been removed, had been uttering slobbery mutters. The very sight of Granny Trotsky, the very sound of her trying to talk as she did at this moment, took away Granny Barnacle's nerve entirely.

She looked at the doctor's face, to read it. "Ah doc, I don't feel too bloody good," she said. "And I just don't feel easy with that bitch in charge. I just feel anything might happen."

"Come, come, the poor woman's overworked," he recited. "We all like to be of help if we can and in any way we can. We are trying to help you, Granny."

When he had gone Granny Barnacle whispered over to Miss Taylor, "Do I look bad, love?"

"No, Granny, you look fine." In fact, Granny Barnacle's face was blotched with dark red.

"Did you hear what doc said about my blood pressure? Do you think it was a lie, just so's I wouldn't make a fuss?"

"Perhaps not."

"For two pins, Granny Taylor, I'd be out of that door and down them stairs if it was the last thing I did and—"

"I shouldn't do that," said Miss Taylor.

"Could they certify me, love?"

"I don't know," said Miss Taylor.

"I'll tell the priest."

"You know what he'll say to you," said Miss Taylor.

"Offer it bloodywell up for the Holy Souls."

"I daresay."

"It's a hard religion, Granny Taylor. If it wasn't that my mother was R.C. I would never of—"

"I know a lady—" It was then Miss Taylor had said,

rashly, "I know a lady who knows another lady who is on the management committee of this hospital. It may take some time but I will see what I can do to get them to transfer Sister Burstead."

"God bless you, Granny Taylor."

"I can't promise. But I'll try. I shall have to be tactful."

"You hear that?" said Granny Barnacle to everyone in the ward. "You hear what Granny Taylor's goin' to do?"

Miss Taylor was not very disappointed with her first effort at sounding Dame Lettie. It was a beginning. She would keep on at Dame Lettie. There was also, possibly, Alec Warner. He might be induced to speak to Tempest Sidebottome who sat on the management committee of the hospital. It might even be arranged without blame to dreary Sister Burstead.

"Didn't your Dame promise nothing definite then?" said Granny Barnacle.

"No, it will take time."

"Will it be done before the winter?"

"I hope so."

"Did you tell her what she done to Granny Duncan?"

"Not exactly."

"You should of. Strikes me you're not on our side entirely, Granny Taylor. I seem to remember that face somehow."

"Whose face?"

"That Dame's face."

The difficulty was, Miss Taylor reflected, she could not feel the affair to be pre-eminently important. Sometimes she would have liked to say to the grannies, "What if your fears were correct? What if we died next winter?" Sometimes she did say to them, "Some of us may die next winter in any case. It is highly probable." Granny Valvona would reply, "I'm ready to meet my God, any time." And Granny Barnacle would stoutly add, "But not before time."

"You must keep on at your friend, Granny Taylor," said Granny Duncan, who, among all the grannies, most irritated Sister Burstead. Granny Duncan had cancer. Miss Taylor often wondered if the sister was afraid of cancer.

"I seem to remember that Dame's face," Granny Barnacle kept on. "Was she ever much round Holborn way of an evening?"

"I don't think so," said Miss Taylor.

"She might be an old customer of mine," said Granny Barnacle.

"I think she had her papers sent."

"Did she go out to work, this Dame?"

"Well, not to a job. But she did various kinds of committee work. That sort of thing."

Granny Barnacle turned over the face of Dame Lettie in her mind. "Was it charity work you said she did?"

"That kind of thing," said Miss Taylor. "Nothing special."

Granny Barnacle looked at her suspiciously, but Miss Taylor would not be drawn, nor say that Dame Lettie had been a Prison Visitor at Holloway from her thirtieth year until it became too difficult for her, with her great weight and breathlessness, to climb the stairs.

"I will keep on at Dame Lettie," she promised.

It was Sister Burstead's day off, and a nurse whistled as she brought in the first supper tray.

Granny Barnacle commented in a hearty voice,

> "A whistling woman, a crowing hen,
> Is neither fit for God nor man."

The nurse stopped whistling and gave Granny Barnacle a close look, dumped the tray and went to fetch another.

Granny Trotsky attempted to raise her head and say something.

"Granny Trotsky wants something," said Granny Duncan.

"What you want, Granny?"

"She is saying," said Miss Taylor, "that we shouldn't be unkind to the nurses just because—"

"Unkind to the nurses! What they goin' to do when the winter—"

Miss Taylor prayed for grace. Is there no way, she thought, for them to forget the winter? Can't they go back to making their wills every week?

In the course of the night Granny Trotsky died as the result of the bursting of a small blood-vessel in her brain, and her spirit returned to God who gave it.

Chapter Five

Mrs. Anthony knew instinctively that Mrs. Pettigrew was a kindly woman. Her instinct was wrong. But the first few weeks after Mrs. Pettigrew came to the Colstons' to look after Charmian she sat in the kitchen and told Mrs. Anthony of her troubles.

"Have a fag," said Mrs. Anthony, indicating with her elbow the packet on the table while she poured strong tea. "Everything might be worse."

Mrs. Pettigrew said, "It couldn't very well be worse. Thirty years of my life I gave to Mrs. Lisa Brooke. Everyone knew I was to get that money. Then this Guy Leet turns up to claim. It wasn't any marriage, that wasn't. Not a proper marriage." She pulled her cup of tea towards her and thrusting her head close to Mrs. Anthony's, told her in what atrocious manner and for what long-ago reason, Guy Leet had been incapable of consummating his marriage with Lisa Brooke.

Mrs. Anthony swallowed a large sip of her tea, the cup of which she held in both hands, and breathed back into the cup while the warm-smelling steam spread comfortingly over her nose. "Still," she said, "a husband's a husband. By law."

"Lisa never recognised him as such," said Mrs. Pettigrew. "No one knew about the marriage with Guy Leet, until she died, the little swine."

"I thought you says she was all right," said Mrs. Anthony.

"Guy Leet," said Mrs. Pettigrew. "He's the little swine."

"Oh, I see. Well the courts will have something to say to that, dear, when it comes up. Have a fag."

"You're making me into a smoker, Mrs. Anthony. Thanks, I will. But you should try to cut them down, they aren't too good for you."

"Twenty a day since I was twenty-five and seventy yesterday," said Mrs. Anthony.

"Seventy! Gracious, you'll be—"

"Seventy years of age yesterday."

"Oh, seventy. Isn't it time you had a rest then? I don't envy you with this lot," Mrs. Pettigrew indicated with her head the kitchen door, meaning the Colstons residing beyond it.

"Not so bad," said Mrs. Anthony. "*He's* a bit tight, but *she's* nice. I like *her*."

"He's tight with the money?" said Mrs. Pettigrew.

Mrs. Anthony said, "Oh very," swivelling her eyes towards her companion to fix the remark.

Mrs. Pettigrew patted her hair which was thick, dyed black and well cut, as Lisa had made her wear it. "How old," she said, "would you say I was Mrs. Anthony?"

Mrs. Anthony, still sitting, pushed back in her chair the better to view Mrs. Pettigrew. She looked at the woman's feet in their suède black shoes, her tight good legs—no veins, her encased hips and good bust. Mrs. Anthony then put her head sideways to regard, from an angle of fifteen degrees, Mrs. Pettigrew's face. There were lines from nose to mouth, a small cherry-painted mouth. Only the beginnings of one extra chin. Two lines across the brow. The eyes were dark and clear, the nose firm and broad. "I should say," said Mrs. Anthony, folding her arms, "you was sixty-four abouts."

The unexpectedness of Mrs. Pettigrew's gentle voice was due to her heavily-marked appearance. It was gentler still as she said to Mrs. Anthony, "Add five years."

"Sixty-nine. You don't look it," said Mrs. Anthony. "Of course you've had the time and money to look after yourself and powder your face. You should of been in business."

In fact, Mrs. Pettigrew was seventy-three, but she did not at all look the age under her make-up.

She drew her hand across her forehead, however, and shook her head slowly. She was worried about the money, the court case which would probably drag on and on. Lisa's family were claiming their rights too.

Mrs. Anthony had started washing up.

"Old Warner still in with *her*," she said, "I suppose?"

"Yes," said Mrs. Pettigrew. "He is."

"It takes her off my hands for a while," said Mrs. Anthony.

"I must say," Mrs. Pettigrew said, "when I was with Lisa Brooke I used to be asked in to meet the callers. I mixed with everyone."

Mrs. Anthony started peeling potatoes and singing.

"I'm going in," said Mrs. Pettigrew, rising and brushing down her neat skirt. "Whether she likes it or whether she doesn't, I'd better keep my eye on her in any case, that's what I'm here for."

When Mrs. Pettigrew entered the drawing-room she said, "Oh, Mrs. Colston, I was just wondering if you were tired."

"You may take the tea-things away," said Charmian.

Instead Mrs. Pettigrew rang for Mrs. Anthony, and, as she piled plates on the tray for the housekeeper to take away, she knew Charmian's guest was looking at her.

Charmian said to Mrs. Anthony, "Thank you, Taylor."

Mrs. Pettigrew had met Alec Warner sometimes at Lisa

Brooke's. He smiled at her and nodded. She sat down and took a cigarette out of her black suède bag. Alec lit it. The clatter of Mrs. Anthony's tray faded out as she receded to the kitchen.

"You were telling me . . . ?" Charmian said to her guest.

"Oh yes." He turned his white head and grey face to Mrs. Pettigrew. "I was explaining the rise of democracy in the British Isles. Do you miss Mrs. Brooke?"

"Very much," said Mabel Pettigrew, blowing out a long puff of smoke. She had put on her social manner. "Do continue about democracy," she said.

"When I went to Russia," said Charmian, "the Tsarina sent an escort to—"

"No, Mrs. Colston, just a moment, while Mr. Alec Warner tells us about democracy."

Charmian looked about her strangely for a moment, then said, "Yes, continue about democracy, Eric."

"Not Eric—Alec," said Mrs. Pettigrew.

Alec Warner soothed the air with his old, old steady hand.

"The real rise of democracy in the British Isles occurred in Scotland by means of Queen Victoria's bladder," he said. "There had, you know, existed an idea of democracy, but the real thing occurred through this little weakness of Queen Victoria's."

Mabel Pettigrew laughed with a backward throw of her head. Charmian looked vague. Alec Warner continued slowly as one filling in the time with his voice. His eyes were watchful.

"Queen Victoria had a little trouble with the bladder, you see. When she went to stay at Balmoral in her latter years a number of privies were caused to be built at the backs of little cottages which had not previously possessed privies. This was to enable the Queen to go on her morning drive round the countryside in comfort, and to descend from her carriage from time to time, ostensibly to visit the humble cottagers in their dwellings. Eventually, word went round that Queen Victoria was exceedingly democratic. Of course it was all due to her little weakness. But everyone copied the Queen and the idea spread, and now you see we have a great democracy."

Mrs. Pettigrew laughed for a long time. Alec Warner was gazing like a bird-watcher at Charmian, who plucked at the rug round her knees, waiting to tell her own story.

"When I went to Russia," said Charmian, looking up at him like a child, "the Tsarina sent an escort to meet me at the frontier, but did not send an escort to take me back. That is so like Russia, they make resolutions then get bored. The male peasants lie on the stove all winter. All the way to Russia my fellow-passengers were opening their boxes and going over their belongings. It was spring and . . ."

Mrs. Pettigrew winked at Alec Warner. Charmian stopped and smiled at him. "Have you seen Jean Taylor lately?" she said.

"Not for a week or two. I have been away to Folkestone on my research work. I shall go to see her next week."

"Lettie goes regularly. She says Jean is very happy and fortunate."

"Lettie is—" He was going to say she was a selfish fool, then remembered Mrs. Pettigrew's presence. "Well, you know what I think of Lettie's opinions," he said and waved away the topic with his hand.

And as if the topic had landed on Charmian's lap, she stared at her lap and continued, "If only you had discovered Lettie's character a little sooner. If only . . ."

He rose to leave, for he knew how Charmian's memory was inclined to wake up in the past, in some arbitrary year. She would likely fix on those events, that year 1907, and bring them close up to her, as one might bring a book close to one's eyes. The time of his love affair with Jean Taylor when she was a parlour-maid at the Pipers' before Charmian's marriage, would be like last week to Charmian. And her novelist's mind by sheer habit still gave to those disjointed happenings a shape which he could not accept, and in a way which he thought dishonest. He had been in love with Jean Taylor, he had decided after all to take everyone's advice. He had therefore engaged himself to Lettie. He had broken the engagement when he came to know Lettie better. These were the facts in 1907. By 1912 he had been able to contemplate them without emotion. But dear Charmian made the most of them. She saw the facts as a dramatic sequence reaching its fingers into all his life's work. This interested him so far as it reflected Charmian, though not at all so far as it affected himself. He would, nevertheless, have liked to linger in his chair on that afternoon, in his seventy-ninth year, and listen to Charmian recalling her youth. But he was embarrassed by Mrs. Pettigrew's presence. Her intrusion had irritated him, and he could not, like Charmian, talk on as if she were not present. He looked at Mrs. Pettigrew as she helped him on with his coat in the hall, and thought, An irritating woman. Then he thought, A fine-looking woman, and this was associated with her career at Lisa's as he had glimpsed it at intervals over twenty-six years. He thought about Mabel Pettigrew all the way home across two parks, though he had meant to think about Charmian on that walk. And he reflected upon himself, amazed, since he was nearly eighty and Mrs. Pettigrew a good, he supposed, sixty-five. "Oh," he said to himself, "these erotic throes that come like thieves in the night to steal my High Churchmanship!" Only, he was not a High Churchman—it was no more than a manner of speaking to himself.

He returned to his rooms—which, since they were officially described as "gentleman's chambers," he always denied were a flat—off St. James's Street. He hung his coat, put away his hat and gloves, then stood at the large bow window gazing out as at an imposing prospect, though in reality the window looked down only on the side entrance to a club. He noted the comings and goings of the club porter. The porter of his own chambers came up the narrow street intently reading the back page of an evening paper. With his inward eye, Dr. Warner, the old sociologist, at the same time contemplated Old Age which had been his study since he had turned seventy. Nearly ten years of inquisitive work had gone into the card indexes and files encased in two oak cabinets, one on either side of the window. His approach to the subject was unique; few gerontologists had the ingenuity or the freedom to conduct their investigations on the lines he had adopted. He got about a good deal; he employed agents; his work was, he hoped, valuable; or would be, one day.

His wide desk was bare, but from a drawer he took a thick bound notebook and sat down to write.

Presently he rose to fetch the two boxes of index cards which he used constantly when working at his desk. One of these contained the names of those of his friends and acquaintances, who were over seventy, with details of his relationship to them, and in the case of chance encounters, the circumstances of their meeting. Special sections were devoted to St. Aubrey's home for mental cases in Folkestone where, for ten years, he had been visiting certain elderly patients by way of unofficial research.

Much of the information on this first set of cards was an aid to memory, for, although his memory was still fairly good, he wished to ensure against his losing it: he had envisaged the day when he might take up a card, read the name and wonder, for instance, "Colston—Charmian,—who is Charmian Colston? Charmian Colston . . . I know the name but I can't for the moment think who . . ." Against this possibility was inscribed "Née Piper. Met 1907. *Vide* Ww page . . ." "Ww," stood for *Who's Who*. The page number was inserted in pencil, to be changed every four years when he acquired a new *Who's Who*.

Most of the cards in this category were filled in with small writing on both sides. All of them were, by his instruction, to be destroyed at his death. At the top left-hand corner of each card was a reference letter and number in red ink. These cross-referred to a second set of cards which bore pseudonyms invented by Dr. Warner for each person. (Thus, Charmian was, in the second set of cards, "Gladys.") All these cards in the second set were his real working cards, for these bore the clues to the case-histories. On each was marked a neat network of codes and numbers relating to various passages in the books around the walls, on the subjects of gerontology and senescence, and to the ten years' accumulation of his thick notebooks.

Alec Warner lifted the house phone and ordered grilled turbot. He sat to his desk, opened a drawer and extracted a notebook; this was his current diary which would also be destroyed at his death. In it he noted his afternoon observations of Charmian, Mrs. Pettigrew and himself. "Her mind," he wrote, "has by no means ceased to function, as her husband makes out. Her mind works associatively. At first she went off into a dream, making plucking movements at the rug on her knees. She appeared to be impatient. She did not follow my story at all, but apparently the words 'Queen Victoria' had evoked some other regal figure. As soon as I had finished she embarked upon a reminiscence (which is likely to be true in detail) of her visit to Petrograd to see her father in 1908. (As she spoke, I myself recalled, for the first time since 1908, Charmian's preparations for her journey to Russia. This has been dormant in my memory since then.) I observed that Charmian did not, however, mention the meeting with her father nor the other diplomat whose name I forget, who later committed suicide on her account. Nor did she mention that she was accompanied by Jean Taylor. I have no reason to doubt the accuracy of her memory on the habits of Russian travellers. So far as I recall her actual words were . . ."

He wrote on till his turbot came up.

My Aunt Marcia, he reflected as he ate, was ninety-two, that is seven years older than Charmian, and was still playing a brilliant game of chess to the time of her death. Mrs. Flaxman, wife of the former Rector of Pineville, was seventy-three when she lost her memory completely; twelve years younger than Charmian. Charmian's memory is not completely gone, it is only erratic. He rose from the table and went to his desk to make a note in the margin of his diary where he had written his day's account of Charmian: "*Vide* Mrs. Flaxman."

He returned to his turbot. Ninon de Lenclos of the seventeenth century died at ninety-nine, in full reason and reputed for wit, he reflected.

His wine glass rested a moment on his lip. Goethe, he mused, was older than me when he was writing love poems to young girls. Renoir at eighty-six . . . Titian, Voltaire. Verdi composed *Falstaff* at the age of eighty. But artists are perhaps exceptions.

He thought of the Maud Long Ward where Jean Taylor lay, and wondered what Cicero would make of it. He looked round his shelves. The great Germans on the subject: they were either visionaries or pathologists, largely. To understand the subject, one had to befriend the people, one had to use spies and win allies.

He ate half of what he had been sent. He drank part of half a bottle of wine. He read over what he had written, the account of the afternoon from the time of his arrival at the Colstons' to his walk back across the park with the thoughts, which had taken him by surprise, of Mrs. Pettigrew whose intrusive presence, as he had noted in his diary, had excited him with both moral irritability and erotic feelings. The diary would go into the fire, but his every morning's work was to analyse and abstract from it the data for his case-histories, entering them in the various methodical notebooks. There Charmian would become an impersonal, almost homeless, "Gladys." Mabel Petti-grew "Joan" and he himself "George."

Meantime he put away his cards and his journal and read, for an hour, from one of the fat volumes of New-man's *Life and Letters*. Before he put it down he marked a passage with a pencil:

> I wonder, in old times what people died of. We read, "After this, it was told Joseph that his father was sick." "And the days of David drew nigh that he should die." What were they sick, what did they die, of? And so of the great Fathers. St. Athanasius died past seventy—was his a paralytic seizure? We cannot imitate the Martyrs in their death—but I sometimes feel it would be a comfort if we could associate ourselves with the great Confessor Saints in their illnesses and decline: Pope St. Gregory had the gout, St. Basil had a liver complaint, but St. Gregory Nazianzen? St. Ambrose? St. Augustine and St. Martin died of fevers, proper to old age. . . .

At nine-thirty he took a packet of ten cigarettes from a drawer and went out. He turned into Pall Mall where the road was up and a nightwatchman on duty whom Alec Warner had been visiting each night for a week past. He hoped to get sufficient consistent answers to construct a history. "How old are you? Where do you live? What do you eat? Do you believe in God? Any religion? Did you ever go in for sport? How do you get on with your wife? How old is she? Who? What? Why? How do you feel?"

"Evening," said the man as Alec approached. "Thanks," he said, as he took the cigarettes. He shifted up on the plank by the brazier to let Alec sit down beside him.

Alec warmed his hands.

"How you feeling to-night?" he said.

"Not so bad! How's yourself, guv?"

"Not so bad. How old did you say . . . ?"

"Seventy-five. Sixty-nine to the Council."

"Of course," said Alec.

"Doesn't do to let on too much."

"I'm seventy-nine," coaxed Alec.

"Don't look a day over sixty-five."

Alec smiled into the fire knowing the remark was untrue, and that he did not care how old he looked, and that most people cared. "Where were you born?" said Alec.

A policeman passed and swivelled his eyes towards the two old men without changing the rhythm of his tread. He was not surprised to see the nightwatchman's superior-looking companion. He had seen plenty of odd old birds.

"That young copper," said Alec, "is wondering what we're up to."

The watchman reached for his bottle of tea, and pulled out the cork.

"Got any tips for to-morrow?"

"Gunmetal for the two-thirty. They say Out of Reach for the four-fifteen. Tell me—"

"Gunmetal's even money," said the watchman. "Not worth your trouble."

"How long," said Alec, "do you sleep during the day?"

Charmian had been put to bed. Rough physical handling made her mind more lucid in some ways, more cloudy in others. She knew quite well at this moment that Mrs. Anthony was not Taylor, and Mabel Pettigrew was Lisa Brooke's former housekeeper, whom she disliked.

She lay and resented, and decided against, Mrs. Pettigrew. The woman had had three weeks' trial and had proved unsatisfactory.

Charmian also lay and fancied Mrs. Pettigrew had wronged her, long ago in the past. This was not the case. In reality, it was Lisa Brooke who had blackmailed Charmian, so that she had been forced to pay and pay, although Lisa had not needed the money; she had been forced to lie awake worrying throughout long night hours, and in the end she had been forced to give up her lover Guy Leet, while Guy had secretly married Lisa to satisfy and silence her for Charmian's sake. All this Charmian blamed upon Mrs. Pettigrew, forgetting for the moment that her past tormentor had been Lisa; so bitter was the particular memory and so vicious was her new tormentor. For Mrs. Pettigrew had wrenched Charmian's arm while getting her dress off, had possibly bruised the arm with her hard impatient grasp. "What you need," Mrs. Pettigrew had said, "is a nurse. I am not a nurse."

Charmian felt indignant at the suggestion that she needed a nurse.

She decided to give Mrs. Pettigrew a month's money in the morning and tell her to go. Before Mrs. Pettigrew had switched out the light, Charmian had spoken sharply. "I think, Mrs. Pettigrew—"

"Oh do call me Mabel and be friendly."

"I think, Mrs. Pettigrew, it will not be necessary for you to come in to the drawing-room when I have visitors unless I ring."

"Good*night*," said Mrs. Pettigrew and switched out the light.

Mrs. Pettigrew descended to her sitting-room and switched on the television which had been installed at her request. Mrs. Anthony had gone home. She took up her knitting and sat working at it while watching the screen. She wanted to loosen her stays but was not sure whether Godfrey would look in to see her. During the three weeks of her stay at the Colstons' he had been in to see her on five evenings. He had not come in last night. Perhaps he would come to-night, and she did not wish to be caught untidy-looking. There was indeed a knock at the door, and she bade him come in.

On the first occasion it had been necessary for him to indicate his requirements to her. But now, she perfectly understood. Godfrey, with his thin face outstanding in the dim lamplight, and his excited eyes, placed on the low coffee table a pound note. He then stood, arms dangling and legs apart, like a stage rustic, watching her. Without shifting her posture she raised the hem of her skirt at one side until the top of her stocking and the tip of her garter were visible. Then she went on knitting and watching the television screen. Godfrey gazed at the stocking-top and the glittering steel of the garter-tip for the space of two minutes' silence. Then he pulled back his shoulders as if recalling his propriety, and still in silence, walked out.

After the first occasion Mrs. Pettigrew had imagined, almost with alarm, that his request was merely the preliminary to more daring explorations on his part, but by now she knew with an old woman's relief that this was all he would ever desire, the top of her stocking and the tip of her garter. She took the pound note off the table, put it in her black suède handbag and loosened her stays. She had plans for the future. Meantime a pound was a pound.

Chapter Six

Miss Jean Taylor sat in the chair beside her bed. She never knew, when she sat in her chair, if it was the last time she would be able to sit out of bed. Her arthritis was gradually spreading and digging deep. She could turn her head slowly. So, and with difficulty, she did. Alec Warner shifted his upright chair a little to face her.

She said, "Are you tormenting Dame Lettie?"

The thought crossed his mind, among other thoughts, that Jean's brain might be undergoing a softening process. He looked carefully at her eyes and saw the grey ring round the edge of the cornea, the *arcus senilis*. Nevertheless, it surrounded the main thing, a continuing intelligence amongst the ruins.

Miss Taylor perceived his scrutiny and thought, It is true he is a student of the subject but he is in many ways the same as the rest. How we all watch each other for signs of failure!

"Come, Alec," she said, "tell me."

"Tormenting Lettie?" he said.

She told him about the anonymous telephone calls, then said, "Stop *studying* me, Alec. I am not soft in the brain as yet."

"Lettie must be so," he said.

"No, she isn't, Alec."

"And supposing," he said, "she really has been receiving

these telephone calls. Why do you suggest I am the culprit? I ask as a matter of interest."

"It seems to me likely, Alec. I may be wrong, but it is the sort of thing, isn't it, that you would do for purposes of study? An experiment—"

"It is the sort of thing," he said, "but in this case I doubt if I am the culprit."

"You *doubt.*"

"Of course I doubt. In a court of law, my dear, I would with complete honesty deny the charge. But you know, I can't affirm or deny anything that is within the range of natural possibility."

"Alec, are you the man, or not?"

"I don't know," he said. "If so, I am unaware of it. But I may be a Jekyll and Hyde, may I not? There was a recent case—"

"Because," she said, "if you are the culprit the police will get you."

"They would have to prove the deed. And if they proved it to my satisfaction I should no longer be in doubt."

"Alec," she said, "are you the man behind those phone calls?"

"Not to my knowledge," he said.

"Then," she said, "you are not the man. Is it someone employed by you?"

He did not seem to hear the question, but was watching Granny Barnacle like a naturalist on holiday. Granny Barnacle accepted his attention with obliging submission, as she did when the doctor brought the medical students round her bed, or when the priest brought the Blessed Sacrament.

"Ask her how she is keeping," said Miss Taylor, "since you are staring at her."

"How are you keeping?" said Alec.

"Not too good," said Granny Barnacle. She jerked her

head to indicate the ward dispensaries just beyond the door. "Time there was a change of management," she said.

"Indeed yes," said Alec, and, inclining his head in final acknowledgment, which included the whole of the Maud Long Ward, returned his attention to Jean Taylor.

"Someone," she said, "in your employ?"

"I doubt it."

"In that case," she said, "the man is neither you nor your agent."

When she had first met him, nearly fifty years ago, she had been dismayed when he had expressed these curious "doubts." She had thought him perhaps a little mad. It had not occurred to her till many years later that this was a self-protective manner of speech which he used exclusively when talking to women whom he liked. He never spoke so to men. She had discerned, after these many years, that this whole approach to the female mind, his only way of coping with it, was to seem to derive amusement from it. When Miss Taylor had made this discovery she was glad they had never been married. He was too much masked behind his mocking, paternal attitude—now become a habit—for any proper relationship with a grown woman.

She recalled an afternoon years ago in 1928—long after the love affair—when she had been attending Charmian on a week-end party in the country and Alec Warner was a fellow-guest. One afternoon he had taken Jean Taylor off for a walk—Charmian had been amused—"to question her, as Jean was so reliable in her evidence." Most of their conversation she had forgotten, but she recalled his first question.

"Do you think, Jean, that other people exist?"

She had not at once understood the nature of the question. For a moment she had wondered if his words might in some way refer to that love affair twenty-odd years earlier, and his further words, "I mean, Jean, do you consider that people—the people around us—are real or illusory?" had possibly some personal bearing. But this did not fit with her knowledge of the man. Even at the time of their love relationship he was not the type to proffer the conceit: there is no one in the world but we two; we alone exist. Besides, she who was now walking beside this middle-aged man was herself a woman in her early fifties.

"What do you mean?" she said.

"Only what I say." They had come to a beech wood which was damp from a last night's storm. Every now and then a little succession of raindrops would pelt from the leaves on to his hat or her hat. He took her arm and led her off the main path, so that for all his sober sense, it rapidly crossed her mind that he might be a murderer, a maniac. But she had, the next instant, recalled her fifty years and more. Were they not usually young women who were strangled in woods by sexual maniacs? No, she thought again, sometimes they were women of fifty-odd. The leaves squelched beneath their feet. Her mind flashed messages to itself back and forth. But I know him well, he's Alec Warner. Do I know him, though?—he is odd. Even as a lover he was strange. But he is known everywhere, his reputation . . . Still, some eminent men have secret vices. No one ever finds them out; their very eminence is a protection.

"Surely," he was saying, as he continued to draw her into the narrow, dripping shadows, "you see that here is a respectable question. Given that you believe in your own existence as self-evident, do you believe in that of others? Tell me, Jean, do you believe that I for instance, at this moment, exist?" He peered down at her face beneath the brim of her brown felt hat.

"Where are you taking me?" she said, stopping still.

"Out of these wet woods," he said, "by a short cut. Tell

me, now, surely you understand what I am asking? It's a plain question. . . ."

She looked ahead through the trees and saw that their path was indeed a short cut to the open fields. She realised at once that his question was entirely academic and he was not contemplating murder with indecent assault. And what reason, after all, had she to suspect this? How things do, she thought, come and go through a woman's mind. He was an unusual man.

"I agree," she then said, "that your question can be asked. One does sometimes wonder, perhaps only half-consciously, if other people are real."

"Please," he said, "wonder more than half-consciously about this question. Wonder about it with as much consciousness as you have, and tell me what is your answer."

"Oh," she said, "I think in that case, other people do exist. That's my answer. It's only common sense."

"You have made up your mind too quickly," he said. "Take time and think about it."

They had emerged from the wood and took a path skirting a ploughed field which led to the village. There the church with its steep sloping graveyard stood at the top of the street. Miss Taylor looked over the wall at the graveyard as they passed it. She was not sure now if his words had been frivolous or serious or both; for, even in their younger days—especially during that month of July 1907 at the farmhouse—she had never really known what to make of him, and had sometimes felt afraid.

She looked at the graveyard and he looked at her. He noted dispassionately that her jaw beneath the shade of the hat was more square than it had ever been. As a young woman she had been round-faced and soft; her voice had been extremely quiet, like the voice of an invalid. In middle age she had begun to reveal, in appearance, angular qualities; her voice was deeper; her jaw-line nearly masculine. He was interested in these factors; he supposed he approved of them; he liked Jean. She stopped and leaned over the low stone wall looking at the gravestones.

"This graveyard is a kind of evidence," she said, "that other people exist."

"How do you mean?" he said.

She was not sure. Having said it, she was not sure why. The more she wondered what she had meant the less she knew.

He tried to climb over the wall, and failed. It was a low wall, but still he was not up to it. "I am going on fifty," he said to her without embarrassment, not even with a covering smile, and she remembered how, at the farmhouse in 1907, when he had chanced to comment that they were both past their prime, he being twenty-eight and she thirty-one, she had felt hurt and embarrassed till she realised he meant no harm by it, meaning only to point a fact. And she, catching this habit and tone, had been able to state quite levelly, "We are not social equals," before the month was over.

He brushed the dust of the graveyard wall from his trousers. "I am going on fifty. I should like to look at the gravestones. Let's go in by the gate."

And so they had walked among the graves, stooping to read the names on the stones.

"They are, I quite see, they are," he said, "an indication of the existence of others, for there are the names and times carved in stone. Not a proof, but at least a large testimony."

"Of course," she said, "the gravestones might be hal-lucinations. But I think not."

"There is that to be considered," he said so courteously that she became angry.

"But the graves are at least reassuring," she said, "for why bother to bury people if they don't exist?"

"Yes, oh precisely," he said.

They ambled up the short drive to the house where Lettie, who sat writing at the library window, glanced towards them and then away again. As they entered, Lisa Brooke with her flaming bobbed head, came out. "Hallo, you two," she said, looking sweetly at Jean Taylor. Alec went straight to his room while Miss Taylor went in search of Charmian. On the way, various people encountered and said "Hallo" to her. This party was composed ⨍ a progressive set; they would think nothing of her walk with Alec that summer of 1928 even though some remembered the farmhouse affair of 1907 which had been a little scandal in those days. Only a brigadier, a misfit in the party who had been invited because the host wanted his advice on dairy herds, and who had passed the couple on their walk, later enquired of Lettie in Miss Taylor's hearing, "Who was that lady I passed with Alec? Has she just arrived?" And Lettie, loathing Jean as she did, but wishing to be broad-minded, replied, "Oh, she's Charmian's maid."

"Say what you like about that sort of thing, the other domestics won't like it," commented the brigadier, which was, after all, true.

And yet, Jean Taylor reflected as she sat with Alec in the Maud Long Ward, perhaps it was not all mockery. He may have half-meant the question.

"Be serious," she said, looking down at her twisted arthritic hands.

Alec Warner Looked at his watch.

"Must you be going?" she said.

"Not for another ten minutes. But it'll take me three-quarters of an hour across the parks. I have to keep fairly strictly to my times, you know. I am going on eighty."

"I'm relieved it's not you, Alec—the telephone calls . . ."

"My dear, this has come from Lettie's imagination, surely that is obvious."

"Oh no. The man has twice left a message with Godfrey. 'Tell Dame Lettie,' he said, 'to remember she must die.'"

"Godfrey heard it too?" he said. "Well, I suppose, in that case, it must be a lunatic. How did Godfrey take it? Did he get a fright?"

"Dame Lettie didn't say."

"Oh, do find out what their reactions were. I hope the police don't catch the fellow too soon. One might get some interesting reactions." He rose to leave.

"Oh, Alec—before you go—there was something else I wanted to ask you."

He sat down again and replaced his hat on her locker.

"Do you know Mrs. Sidebottome?"

"Tempest? Ronald's wife. Sister-in-law of Lisa Brooke. Now in her seventy-first year. I first met her on a boat entering the Bay of Biscay in 1930. She was—"

"That's right. She is on the Management Committee of this hospital. The sister in charge of this ward is unsuitable. We all here desire her to be transferred to another ward. Do you want me to go into details?"

"No," he said. "You wish me to talk to Tempest."

"Yes. Make it plain that the nurse in question is simply overworked. There was a fuss about her some time ago, but nothing came of it."

"I cannot speak to Tempest just yet. She went into a nursing home for an operation last week."

"A serious one?"

"A tumour on the womb. But at her age it is, in itself, less serious than in a younger woman."

"Oh well, then you can't do anything for us at present."

"I shall think," he said, "if I know anyone else. Have you approached Lettie on the subject?"

"Oh, yes."

He smiled, and said, "Approach her no more. It is a waste of time. You must seriously think, Jean, of going to that home in Surrey. The cost is not high. Godfrey and I can manage it. I think Charmian would be joining you there soon. Jean, you should have a room of your own."

"Not now," said Miss Taylor. "I shan't move from here. I've made friends here, it's my home."

"See you next Wednesday, my dear," he said, taking his hat and looking round the ward, sharply, at each of the grannies in turn.

"All being well," she said.

Two years ago, when she first came to the ward, she had longed for the private nursing home in Surrey about which there had been too much talk. Godfrey had made a fuss about the cost, he had expostulated in her presence, and had quoted a number of their friends of the progressive set on the subject of the new free hospitals, how superior they were to the private affairs. Alec Warner had pointed out that these were days of transition, that a person of Jean Taylor's intelligence and habits might perhaps not feel at home among the general aged of a hospital.

"If only," he said, "because she is partly what we have made her, we should look after her."

He had offered to bear half the cost of keeping Jean in Surrey. But Dame Lettie had finally put an end to these arguments by coming to Jean with a challenge, "Would you not really, my dear, *prefer* to be independent? After all, you are the public. The hospitals are *yours*. You are entitled . . ." Miss Taylor had replied, "I prefer to go to hospital, certainly." She had made her own arrangements and had left them with the daily argument still in progress concerning her disposal.

Alec Warner had not liked to see her in this ward. The first week he had wanted her to move. In misery she had vacillated. Her pains were increasing, she was not yet resigned to them. There had been further consultations and talking things over. Should she be moved to Surrey? Might not Charmian join her there eventually?

Not now, she thought, after Alec Warner had departed. Granny Valvona had put on her glasses and was searching for the horoscopes. Not now, thought Miss Taylor. Not now that the worst is over.

At first, in the morning light, Charmian forgave Mrs. Pettigrew. She was able, slowly, to walk downstairs by herself. Other movements were difficult and Mrs. Pettigrew had helped her to dress quite gently.

"But," said Mabel Pettigrew to her, "you should get into the habit of breakfast in bed."

"No," said Charmian cheerfully as she tottered round the table, grasping the backs of chairs, to her place. "That would be a bad habit. My morning cup of tea in bed is all that I desire. Good morning, Godfrey."

" 'Lydia May,' " said Godfrey, reading from the paper, " 'died yesterday at her home in Knightsbridge six days before her ninety-second birthday.' "

"A Gaiety Girl," said Charmian. "I well remember."

"You're in good form this morning," Mrs. Pettigrew remarked. "Don't forget to take your pills." She had put the bottle beside Charmian's plate. She now unscrewed the cap and extracted two pills which she laid before Charmian.

"I have had my pills already," said Charmian. "I had them with my morning tea, don't you remember?"

"No," said Mrs. Pettigrew, "you are mistaken, dear. Take your pills."

"She made a fortune," Godfrey remarked. "Retired in 1893 and married money both times. I wonder what she has left?"

"She was before my time, of course," said Mabel Pettigrew.

"Nonsense," said Godfrey.

"I beg your pardon, Mr. Colston, she was before my time. If she retired in 1893 I was only a child in 1893."

"*I* remember her," said Charmian. "She sang most expressively—in the convention of those times you know."

"At the Gaiety?" said Mrs. Pettigrew. "Surely—"

"No, I heard her at a private party."

"Ah, you would be quite a grown girl, then. Take your pills dear." She pushed the two white tablets towards Charmian. Charmian pushed them back and said, "I have already taken my pills this morning. I recall quite clearly. I usually do take them with my early tea."

"Not always," said Mrs. Pettigrew. "Sometimes you forget and leave them on your tray, as you did this morning, actually."

" 'She was the youngest of fourteen children,' " Godfrey read out from the paper, " 'of a strict Baptist family. It was not till her father's death, that, at the age of eighteen she made her début in a small part at the Lyceum. Trained by Ellen Terry and Sir Henry Irving, she left them however for The Gaiety where she became the principal dancer. The then Prince of Wales—' "

"She was introduced to us at Cannes," said Charmian, gaining confidence in her good memory that morning, "wasn't she?"

"That's right," said Godfrey, "it would be about 1910."

"And she stood up on a chair and looked round her and said, 'Gad! The place is stinking with royalty.' Remember we were terribly embarrassed, and—"

"No, Charmian, no. You've got it wrong there. It was one of the Lilly Sisters who stood on a chair. And that was much later. There was nothing like that about Lydia May, she was a different class of girl."

Mrs. Pettigrew placed the two pills a little nearer to Charmian, but said no more about them. Charmian said, "I mustn't exceed my dose," and shakily replaced them in the bottle.

"Charmian, take your pills, my dear," said Godfrey and took a noisy sip from his coffee.

"I have taken two pills already. I remember quite clearly doing so. Four might be dangerous."

Mrs. Pettigrew cast her eyes to the ceiling and sighed.

"What is the use," said Godfrey, "of me paying big doctor's bills if you won't take his stuff?"

"Godfrey, I do not wish to be poisoned by an overdose. Moreover, my own money pays for the bills."

" 'Poisoned,' " said Mrs. Pettigrew, laying down her napkin as if tried beyond endurance. "I ask you."

"Or merely upset," said Charmian. "I do not wish to take the pills, Godfrey."

"Oh well," he said, "if that's how you feel, I must say it makes life damned difficult for all of us, and we simply can't take responsibility if you have an attack through neglecting the doctor's instructions."

Charmian began to cry. "I know you want to put me away in a home."

Mrs. Anthony had just come in to clear the table.

"There," she said. "Who wants to put you in a home?"

"We are a little upset, what with one thing and another," said Mrs. Pettigrew.

Charmian stopped crying. She said to Mrs. Anthony, "Taylor, did you see my early tea-tray when it came down?"

Mrs. Anthony seemed not to grasp the question, for though she had heard it, for some reason she felt it was more complicated than it really was.

Charmian repeated, "Did you see—"

"Now, Charmian," said Godfrey, foreseeing some possible contradiction between Mrs. Anthony's reply and Mrs. Pettigrew's previous assertion. In this, he was concerned overwhelmingly to prevent a conflict between the two women. His comfort, the whole routine of his life, depended on retaining Mrs. Anthony. Otherwise he might have to give up the house and go to some hotel. And Mrs. Pettigrew having been acquired, she must be retained; otherwise Charmian would have to go to a home. "Now, Charmian, we don't want any more fuss about your pills," he said.

"What did you say about the tea-tray, Mrs. Colston?"

"Was there anything on it when it came down from my room?"

Mrs. Pettigrew said, "Of course there was nothing on the tray. I replaced the pills you had left on it in the bottle."

"There was a cup and saucer on the tray. Mrs. Pettigrew brought it down," said Mrs. Anthony, contributing what accuracy she could to questions which still confused her.

Mrs. Pettigrew started noisily loading the breakfast dishes on to Mrs. Anthony's tray. She said to Mrs. Anthony, "Come, my dear, we've work to do."

Mrs. Anthony felt she had somehow failed Charmian, and so, as she followed Mrs. Pettigrew out of the door she pulled a face at her.

When they were gone Godfrey said, "See the fuss you've caused. Mrs. Pettigrew was quite put out. If we lose her—"

"Ah," said Charmian,. "you are taking your revenge, Eric."

"I am not Eric," he said.

"But you are taking your revenge." Fifteen years ago, in her seventy-first year, when her memory had started slightly to fail, she had realised that Godfrey was turning upon her as one who had been awaiting his revenge. She did not think he was himself aware of this. It was an instinctive reaction to the years of being a talented, celebrated woman's husband, knowing himself to be reaping continually in her a harvest which he had not sown.

Throughout her seventies Charmian had not reproached him with his bullying manner. She had accepted his new domination without comment until her weakness had become so marked that she physically depended on him more and more. It was then, in her eighties, that she started frequently to say what, in the past, she would have considered unwise: "You are taking your revenge."

And on this occasion, as always, he replied, "What revenge for *what?*" He really did not know. He saw only that she was beginning to look for persecution: poison, revenge; what next? "You are getting into a state of imagining that all those around you are conspiring against you," he said.

"Whose fault is it," she said with a jolting sharpness, "if I am getting into such a state?"

This question exasperated him, partly because he sensed a deeper sanity in it than in all her other accusations, and partly because he could not answer it. He felt himself to be a heavily burdened man.

Later in the morning, when the doctor called, Godfrey stopped him in the hall.

"She is damn difficult to-day, Doctor."

"Ah well," said the doctor, "it's a sign of life."

"Have to see about a home if she goes on like this."

"It might be a good idea, if only she can be brought round to liking it," said the doctor. "The scope for regular attention is so much better in a nursing home, and I have known cases far more advanced than your wife's which have improved tremendously once they have been moved to a really comfortable home. How are you feeling yourself?"

"Me? Well, what can you expect with all the domestic worries on my shoulders?" said Godfrey. He pointed to the door of the garden-room where Charmian was waiting. "You'd better go on in," he said, being disappointed of the sympathy and support he had hoped for, and vaguely put out by the doctor's talk of Charmian's possible improvement in health, should she be sent to a home.

The doctor's hand was on the door knob. "I shouldn't worry too much about domestic matters," he said. "Go out as much as possible. Your wife, as I say, may buck up tremendously if we have to move her. It sometimes proves a stimulus. Of course, at her age . . . her resistance . . . but there's a chance that she may still get about again. It is largely neurasthenia. She has extraordinary powers of recovery, almost as if she had some secret source. . . ."

Godfrey thought: This is his smarm. Charmian has a secret source, and I pay the bills. He said explosively, "Well sometimes I feel she deserves to be sent away. Take this morning for instance—"

"Oh *deserves*," said the doctor, "we don't recommend nursing-homes as a punishment, you know."

"Bloody man," said Godfrey in the doctor's hearing and before he had properly got into the room where Charmian waited.

Immediately the doctor had entered through the door so did Mrs. Pettigrew through the french windows. "Pleasant for the time of year," she said.

"Yes," said the doctor. "Good morning, Mrs. Colston. How do you feel to-day?"

"We wouldn't," said Mrs. Pettigrew, "take our pills this morning, Doctor, I'm afraid."

"Oh, that doesn't matter," he said.

"I did take them," said Charmian. "I took them with my early tea, and they tried to force me to take more at breakfast. I know I took them with my early tea, and just suppose I had taken a second dose—"

"It wouldn't really have mattered," he said.

"But surely," said Mrs. Pettigrew, "it is always dangerous to exceed a stated dose."

"Just try to keep a careful check—a set routine for medicines in future," he said to Mrs. Pettigrew. "Then neither of you will make a mistake."

"There was no mistake on my part," said Mrs. **Pettigrew**. "There is nothing wrong with my memory."

"In that case," said Charmian, "we must question your *intentions* in trying to give me a second dose. Taylor knows I took my pills as I always do. I did not leave them on the tray."

The doctor said as he took her pulse, "Mrs. Pettigrew, if you would excuse us for a moment . . ."

She went out with a deep loud weary sigh, and, in the kitchen, stood and berated Mrs. Anthony for "taking that mad-woman's part this morning."

"She isn't," said Mrs. Anthony, "a mad-woman. She's always been good to me."

"No, she isn't mad," said Mrs. Pettigrew, "you are right. She's cunning and sly. She isn't as feeble as she makes out, let me tell you. I've watched her when she didn't know I was watching. She can move about quite easily when she likes."

"Not when she likes," said Mrs. Anthony, "but when she feels up to it. After all, I've been here nine years, haven't I? Mrs. Colston is a person who needs a lot of understanding, she has her off days and her on days. No one understands her like I do."

"It's preposterous," said Mrs. Pettigrew, "a woman of my position being accused of attempts to poison. Why, if I was going to do that I should go about it a very different way, I assure you, to giving her overdoses in front of everybody."

"I bet you would," said Mrs. Anthony. "Mind out my way," she said, for she was sweeping the floor unnecessarily.

"Mind how you talk to me, Mrs. Anthony."

"Look," said Mrs. Anthony, "my husband goes on at me about this job now he's at home all day, he doesn't like me being out. I only do it for that bit of independence and it's what I've always done my married life. But we can do on the pension now I'm seventy and the old man sixty-eight, and any trouble from you, let me tell you I'm leaving here. I managed *her* myself these nine years and we got on without you interfering and making trouble."

"I shall speak to Mr. Colston," said Mrs. Pettigrew, "and inform him of what you say."

"Him," said Mrs. Anthony. "Go on and speak to him. I don't reckon much of him. She's the one that I care for, not *him*." Mrs. Anthony followed this with an insolent look.

"What do you mean by that exactly?" said Mrs. Pettigrew. "What exactly do you mean?"

"You work it out for yourself," said Mrs. Anthony. "I'm busy with their luncheon."

Mrs. Pettigrew went in search of Godfrey who was, however, out. She went by way of the front door round to the french windows, and through them. She saw that the doctor had left and Charmian was reading a book. She was filled with a furious envy at the thought that, if she herself were to take the vapours, there would not be any expensive doctor to come and give her a kind talk and an injection no doubt, and calm her down so that she could sit and read a book after turning the household upside down.

Mrs. Pettigrew went upstairs to look round the bedrooms, to see if they were all right and tidy, and in reality to simmer down and look round. She was annoyed with herself for letting go at Mrs. Anthony. She should have kept aloof. But it had always been the same—even when she had been with Lisa Brooke—when she had to deal with lower domestics she became too much one of them. It was kindness of heart, but it was weak. She reflected that she had really started off on the wrong foot with Mrs. Anthony; that, when she had first arrived, she should have kept her distance with the woman and refrained from confidences. And now she had lowered herself to an argument with Mrs. Anthony. These thoughts overwhelmed Mrs.

Pettigrew with that sense of having done a foolish thing against one's interests, which in some people stands for guilt. And in this frame of heart she repented, and decided, as she stood by Charmian's neatly-made bed, to establish her position more solidly in the household, and from now on to treat Mrs. Anthony with remoteness.

A smell of burning food rose up the well of the stairs and into Charmian's bedroom. Mrs. Pettigrew leaned over the banister and sniffed. Then she listened. No sound came from the kitchen, no sound of hurried removal of pots from the gas jets. Mrs. Pettigrew came half-way down the stairs and listened. From the small garden-room where Charmian had been sitting came voices. Mrs. Anthony was in there, recounting her wrongs to Charmian while the food was burning in the oven and the potatoes burning dry and the kettle burning on the stove. Mrs. Pettigrew turned back up the stairs, and up one more flight to her own room. There she got from a drawer a box of keys. She selected four and putting them in the black suède handbag which, perhaps by virtue of her office, she always carried about the house, descended to Charmian's bedroom. Here, she tried the keys one by one in the lid of Charmian's bureau. The third fitted. She did not glance within the desk, but locked the lid again. With the same key she tried the drawers. It did not fit them. She placed the key carefully in a separate compartment of her handbag and tried the other keys. None fitted the drawers. She went to the landing, where the smell of burning had become alarming, and listened. Mrs. Anthony had not yet left Charmian, and it was clear to Mrs. Pettigrew that when she did, there would be enough to keep her busy for ten minutes more. She took from her bag a package of chewing gum, and unwrapped it. There were five strips of gum. She put the paper with three of the pieces back in her bag and two pieces of gum in her mouth. She sat on a chair near the open door and chewed for a few seconds. Then she wet the tips of her fingers with her tongue, took the soft gum from her mouth and flattened it. She next wet the surface of the gum with her tongue and applied it to the keyhole of one of the drawers. She withdrew it quickly and put it on Charmian's bedside table to set. She took two more pieces of gum, and having chewed them as before, moistened the lump and applied it to the keyhole of another drawer. She slung back her bag up to her wrist and holding the two pieces of gum with their keyhole impressions, between the finger and thumb of each hand, walked up the flight of stairs to her bedroom. She placed the hardened gum carefully in a drawer, locked the drawer, and set off downstairs, through the houseful of smoke and smell.

Mrs. Anthony came rushing out of the garden-room just as Mrs. Pettigrew appeared on the first flight of stairs.

"Do I," said Mrs. Pettigrew, "smell burning?"

By the time she reached the foot of the stairs Mrs. Anthony was already in the kitchen holding the smoking raging saucepan under the tap. A steady blue cloud was pouring through the cracks of the oven door. Mrs. Pettigrew opened the door of the oven, and was driven back by a rush of smoke. Mrs. Anthony dropped her potato saucepan and ran to the oven.

"Turn off the gas," she said to Mrs. Pettigrew. "Oh, the pie!"

Mrs. Pettigrew, spluttering, approached the oven and turned off the gas taps, then she ran coughing from the kitchen and went in to Charmian.

"Do I smell burning?" said Charmian.

"The pie and potatoes are burned to cinders."

"Oh, I shouldn't have kept Taylor talking," said Charmian. "The smell is quite bad, isn't it? Shall we open the windows?"

Mrs. Pettigrew opened the french windows and like a

ghost, a stream of blue smoke obligingly wafted out into the garden.

"Godfrey," said Charmian, "will be so cross. What is the time?"

"Twenty past," said Mrs. Pettigrew.

"Eleven?"

"No, twelve."

"Oh, dear. Do go and see how Mrs. Anthony is getting on. Godfrey will be in any moment."

Mrs. Pettigrew remained by the french windows. "I expect," she said, "Mrs. Anthony is losing her sense of smell. She is quite aged for seventy, isn't she? What I would call an *old* seventy. You would have thought she could have smelt the burning long before it got to this stage." A sizzling sound came round the back of the house from the kitchen where Mrs. Anthony was drenching everything with water.

"*I* smelt nothing," said Charmian. "I'm afraid I kept her talking. Poor soul, she is—"

"There's Mr. Colston," said Mrs. Pettigrew, "just come in." She went out to the hall to meet him.

"What the hell is burning?" he said. "Have you had a fire?"

Mrs. Anthony came out of the kitchen and gave him an account of what had happened, together with accusations, complaints, and a fortnight's notice.

"I shall go and make an omelette," said Mrs. Pettigrew, and casting her eyes to heaven for Godfrey to see behind Mrs. Anthony's back, disappeared into the kitchen to cope with the disorder.

But Godfrey would eat nothing. He told Charmian, "This is all your fault. The household is upside down just because you argued about your pills this morning."

"An overdose may have harmed me, Godfrey. I was not to know the pills were harmless."

"There was no question of overdose. I should like to

know *why* the pills were harmless. I mean to say, if the fellow prescribes two and you may just as well take four, what sort of a prescription is that, what good are the pills to you? I'm going to pay the bill and tell him not to come back. We'll get another doctor."

"I shall refuse to see another doctor."

"Mrs. Anthony has given notice, do you realise what that means?"

"I shall persuade her to stay," said Charmian. "She has been under great strain this morning."

He said, "Well, I'm going out again. This place is stinking." He went to get his coat and returned to say, "Be sure to get Mrs. Anthony to change her mind." From past experience, he knew that only Charmian could do it. "It's the least you can do after all the trouble. . . ."

Mrs. Pettigrew and Mrs. Anthony sat eating their omelette with their coats on, since it was necessary to have all windows open. In the course of the meal Mrs. Pettigrew quarrelled with Mrs. Anthony again, and was annoyed with herself afterwards for it. If only, she thought guiltily, I could keep a distance, that would be playing my cards.

Mrs. Anthony sat with Charmian all afternoon, while Mrs. Pettigrew, with the sense of performing an act of reparation, took her two pieces of chewing gum, each marked with a clear keyhole impression, to a person she knew at Camberwell Green.

Chapter Seven

There was a chill in the air, but Godfrey walked on the sunny side of the street. He had parked his car in a turning off King's Road outside a bombed building, so that anyone who recognised it would not be able to guess particularly why it was there. Godfrey had, for over three years now, been laboriously telling any of his acquaintance who lived near Chelsea, that his oculist was in Chelsea, his lawyer was in Chelsea, and that he frequently visited a chiropodist in Chelsea. The more alert of his acquaintance had sometimes wondered why he stated these facts emphatically and so often—almost every time they met him. But he was, after all, over eighty and, one supposed, inclined to waffle about the merest coincidences.

Godfrey himself was of the feeling that one can never be too careful. Having established an oculist, a lawyer and a chiropodist in the neighbourhood to account for his frequent appearances in Chelsea, he still felt it necessary to park his car anonymously, and walk the rest of the way, by routes expressly devious, to Tite Street where, in a basement flat, Olive Mannering, grand-daughter of Percy Mannering, the poet, resided.

He looked to right and left at the top of the area steps. The coast was clear. He looked to right again, and descended. He pushed the door open and called, "Hello, there."

"Mind the steps," Olive called from the front room on

the left. There were three more steps to descend within the doorway. Godfrey walked down carefully, and found his way along the passage into a room of many lights. Olive's furnishings were boxy and modern, coloured with a predominance of yellow. She herself was fairly drab in comparison. She was twenty-four. Her skin was pale with a touch of green. She had a Spanish look, with slightly protruding, large eyes. Her legs, full at the calves, were bare. She sat on a stool and warmed these legs by a large electric fire while reading the *Manchester Guardian*.

"Goodness, it's you," she said, as Godfrey entered. "Your voice is exactly like Eric's. I thought it was Eric."

"Is he in London, then?" said Godfrey, looking round the room suspiciously, for there had been an afternoon when he had called on Olive and met his son Eric there. Godfrey, however, had immediately said to Olive,

"I wonder if you have your grandfather's address? I wish to get in touch with him."

Olive had started to giggle. Eric had said "Ha—hum" very meaningly and, as Olive told him later, disrespectfully.

"I wish to get in touch with him in connection with," said Godfrey, glaring at his son, "some poetry."

Olive was a fair-minded girl in so far as she handed over to Eric most of the monthly allowances she obtained from Godfrey. She felt this was only Eric's due, since his father had allowed him nothing for nearly ten years past, Eric being now fifty-six.

"Is Eric in London?" said Godfrey again.

"He is," said Olive.

"I'd better not stop," said Godfrey.

"He won't be coming here to-day," she said. "I'll just go and put my stockings on," she said. "Would you like some tea?"

"Yes, all right," said Godfrey. He folded his coat double and laid it on the divan-bed. On top of it he placed his hat. He looked to see if the curtains were properly drawn across the basement window. He sat down with a thump in one of the yellow chairs which were too low-built for his liking, and picked up the *Manchester Guardian*. Sometimes, while he waited, he looked at the clock.

Olive returned, wearing stockings and carrying a tea-tray.

"Goodness, are you in a hurry?" she said as she saw Godfrey looking at the clock. He was not in a hurry, exactly. He was not yet sure of the cause of his impatience that afternoon.

Olive placed the tray on a low table and sat on her low stool. She lifted the hem of her skirt to the point where her garter met the top of her stockings, and with legs set together almost primly sideways, she poured out the tea.

Godfrey did not know what had come over him. He stared at the garter-tips, but somehow did not experience his usual satisfaction at the sight. He looked at the clock.

Olive, passing him his tea, noticed that his attention was less fixed on her garter-tips than was customary.

"Anything the matter, Godfrey?" she said.

"No," he said, and took his tea. He sipped it, and stared again at the tops of her stockings, evidently trying hard to be mesmerised.

Olive lit a cigarette and watched him. His eyes did not possess their gleam.

"What's the matter?" she said.

He was wondering himself what was the matter. He sipped his tea.

"Running a car," he remarked, "is a great expense."

She burst into a single laugh and said, "Oh, go on."

"Cost of living," he muttered.

She covered up her garter-tops with her skirt and sat hugging her knees, as one whose efforts are wasted. He did not seem to notice.

"Did you see in the paper," she said, "about the preacher giving a sermon on his hundredth birthday?"

"Which paper, where?" he said, reaching out for the *Manchester Guardian*.

"It was the *Mirror*," she said. "I wonder what I've done with it? He said anyone can live to a hundred if they keep God's laws and remain young in spirit. Goodness."

"The government robbers," he said, "won't let you keep young in spirit. Sheer robbery."

Olive was not listening, or she would not have chosen that moment to say, "Eric's in a bad way, you know."

"He's always in a bad way. What's the matter now?"

"The usual," she said.

"What usual?"

"Money," she said.

"I can't do more for Eric. I've done more than enough for Eric. Eric has ruined me."

Then, as in a revelation, he realised what had put him off Olive's garters that afternoon. It was this money question, this standing arrangement with Olive. It had been going on for three years. Pleasant times, of course . . . One had possibly gained . . . but now, Mabel Pettigrew—what a find! Quite pleased with a mere tip, a pound, and a handsome woman, too. All this business of coming over to Chelsea. No wonder one was feeling put out, especially as one could not easily extricate oneself from an arrangement such as that with Olive. Moreover . . .

"I'm not so strong these days," he commented. "My doctor thinks I'm going about too much."

"Oh?" said Olive.

"Yes. Must keep indoors more."

"Goodness," said Olive. "You are wonderful for your age. A man like you could never stay indoors all day."

"Well," he admitted, "there is that to it." He was moved to look longingly at her legs at the point where, beneath her dress, the tip of her garter would meet the top of her stockings, but she made no move to reveal them.

"You tell your doctor," she said, "to go to hell. What did you see the doctor about, anyway?"

"Just aches and pains, my dear, nothing serious of course."

"Many a younger man," she said, "is riddled with aches and pains. Take Eric, for instance—"

"Feeling his age, is he?"

"I'll say he is. Goodness."

Godfrey said, "Only himself to blame. No, I'm wrong, I blame his mother. From the moment that boy was born, she—"

He leaned back in his chair with his hands crossed above his stomach. Olive closed her eyes and relaxed while his voice proceeded into the late afternoon.

Godfrey reached his car outside the bomb site. He had felt cramped when he rose from that frightful modern chair of Olive's. One had talked on, and remained longer than one had intended. He climbed stiffly into the car and slammed the door, suddenly reproached by the more dignified personality he now had to resume.

Why does one behave like this, why? he asked himself as he drove into King's Road and along it. Why does one do these things? he thought, never defining, however, exactly what things. How did it start, at what point in one's life does one find oneself doing things like this? And he felt resentful against Charmian who had been, all her life with him, regarded by everyone as the angelic partner endowed with sensibility and refined tastes. As for oneself, of Colston's Breweries, one had been the crude fellow, tolerated for her sake, and thus driven into carnality, as it were. He felt resentful against Charmian, and raced home to see if she had made everything all right after upsetting Mrs. Anthony and Mrs. Pettigrew. He took out his watch. It was seven and a half minutes to six. Home,

home, for a drink. Funny how Olive never seemed to have any drinks in her flat. Couldn't afford it, she said. Funny she couldn't afford it; what did she do with her money, one wondered.

At half-past six Alec Warner arrived at Olive's. She poured him a gin and tonic which he placed on a table beside his chair. He took a hard-covered notebook from his briefcase. "How are things?" he said, leaning his large white head against the yellow chair-back.

"Guy Leet," she said, "has been diagnosed again for his neck. It's a rare type of rheumatism, it sounds like *tortoise*."

"Torticollis?" said Alec Warner.

"That's it."

Alec Warner made a note in his book. "Trust him," he said, "to have a rare rheumatism. How are things otherwise?"

"Dame Lettie Colston has changed her will again."

"Lovely," he said, and made a note. "What way has she changed it?"

"Eric is out again, for one. Martin is put in again. That's the other nephew in Africa."

"She thinks Eric is responsible for the telephone calls, does she?"

"She suspects everyone. Goodness. This is her way of testing Eric. That ex-detective is out."

"Chief Inspector Mortimer?"

"Yes. She thinks it might be him. Funny, it is. She has no sooner got him working privately on the case, than she thinks it might be him."

"How old is Mortimer?" he asked.

"Nearly seventy."

"I know. But when exactly will he be seventy? Did you enquire?"

"I'll find out exactly," said Olive.

"Always find out exactly," he said.

"I think," said Olive, defending her lapse as best she could, "he'll be seventy quite soon—early next year, I think."

"Find out exactly, dear," said Warner. "Meantime he is not one of us. We'll come to *him* next year."

"She thinks you may be the culprit," said Olive. "Are you?"

"I doubt it," he said wearily. He had received a letter from Dame Lettie asking the same question.

"How you talk," she said. "Well, I wouldn't have put it past you."

"Mrs. Anthony," she said, "had a row with Mrs. Pettigrew this morning and is threatening to leave. Charmian accused Mrs. Pettigrew of trying to poison her."

"That's *very* hot news," he said. "Godfrey has been here to-day, I gather?"

"Oh yes. He was rather odd to-day. Something's put him off his stroke."

"Not interested in garters to-day?"

"No, but he was trying hard. He said his doctor doesn't want him to go out and about so much. I didn't know whether to take that as a hint, or—"

"Mrs. Pettigrew—have you thought of *her?*"

"Oh goodness," said Olive, "I haven't." She smiled widely and placed a hand over her mouth.

"Try to find out," he said.

"Oh dear," said Olive, "no more fivers for poor old Eric. I can see it coming. Do you think Mrs. Pettigrew has it in her?"

"I do," said Alec, writing his notes.

"There's a bit in the paper in the kitchen," said Olive, "about a preacher preaching on his hundredth birthday."

"What paper?"

"The *Mirror.*"

"My press-cutting agency covers the *Mirror.* It's only

the out-of-the-way papers they sometimes overlook. But thanks all the same. Always tell me of anything like that, just in case. Keep on the look out."

"O.K.," said Olive, and sipped her drink, watching the old veined hand moving its pen steadily, in tiny writing, over the page.

He looked up. "How frequently would you say," he said, "he passes water?"

"Oh goodness, it didn't say anything about that in the *Mirror*."

"You know I mean Godfrey Colston."

"Well, he was here about two hours and he went twice. Of course he had two cups of tea."

"Is twice the average when he comes here?"

"I can't remember. I think—"

"You must try to remember everything exactly, my dear," said Alec. "You must watch, my dear, and pray. It is the only way to be a scholar, to watch and to pray."

"Me a scholar, goodness. He had patches of red on the cheekbones to-day, more so than usual."

"Thank you," said Alec, and made a note. "Notice everything, Olive," he looked up and said, "for only you can observe him in relation to yourself. When I meet him, you understand, he is a different personality."

"I'll bet," she said, and laughed.

He did not laugh. "Be sure to find out all you can on his next visit in case he deserts you for Mrs. Pettigrew. When do you expect to see him again?"

"Friday, I suppose."

"There is someone," he said, "tapping at the window behind me."

"Is there? It must be Granpa, he always does that." She rose to go to the door.

Alec said quickly, "Tell me, does he tap on the window of his own accord or have you asked him to announce himself in that way?"

"He does it of his own accord. He always has tapped at the window."

"Why? Do you know?"

"No—no idea."

Alec bent once more with his pen over his book, and recorded the facts which he would later analyse down to their last, stubborn elements.

Olive fetched in Percy Mannering who, on entering the room, addressed Alec Warner without preliminaries, waving in front of him a monthly magazine of a literary nature, on the cover of which was stamped in bold lettering, "Kensington Public Libraries."

"Guy Leet," roared Percy, "that moron has published part of his memoirs in which he refers to Ernest Dowson as 'that weak-kneed wailer of Gallic weariness afflicted with an all-too-agonised afflatus.' He is fantastically wrong about Dowson. Ernest Dowson was the spiritual and aesthetic child of Swinburne, Tennyson and Verlaine. You can hear all their voices and Dowson was something of a French scholar and quite obviously under the spell of Verlaine as well as Tennyson and Swinburne, and very much in Arthur Symons' circle. He is fantastically wrong about Ernest Dowson."

"How are you keeping?" said Alec, having risen from his chair.

"Guy Leet was never a good theatre critic, and he was a worse novel critic. He knows nothing about poetry, he has no right to touch the subject. Can't someone stop him?"

"What else," said Alec, "does he say in his memoir?"

"A lot of superficiality about how he attacked a novel of Henry James's and then met James outside the Athenæum one day and James was talking about his conscience as an artist and Guy's conscience as a critic, and that whatever was actually committed to print—"

"Let the fire see the people, Granpa," said Olive, for Percy was standing back-to-fire straddling and monopolising it. Alec Warner had closed and put away his note-book.

The poet did not move.

"That's because Henry James is fashionable to-day, that's why he writes about Henry James. Whereas he jeers at poor Ernest— If you're pouring that brandy for me, Olive, it's too much. Half of that— Ernest Dowson, a supreme lyricist." He took the glass, which he held with a shaky claw-like hand, and while taking his first sip seemed of a sudden to forget Ernest Dowson.

He said to Alec, "I didn't see you at Lisa's funeral."

"Sit down, Granpa," said Olive. She worked him into a chair.

"I missed it," said Alec, watching Percy's lean profile with concentration. "I was in Folkestone at the time."

"It was a fearful and thrilling experience," said Percy.

"In what way?" said Alec.

The old poet smiled. He cackled from the depth of his throat, and the memory of Lisa's cremation seemed to be refracted from his mind's eye to the avid eyes in his head. As he talked, the eyes of Alec feasted on him, in turn.

Percy stayed on with his grand-daughter after Alec Warner had left. She prepared a supper of mushrooms and bacon which they ate off trays perched on their knees. She watched him while he ate. He gnawed with his few teeth at the toasted bread, but got through all of it, even the difficult crusts.

He looked up as he managed the last small rim of crust and saw her watching him. When he had finished all, he remarked, "Final perseverance."

"What you say, Granpa?"

"Final perseverance is the doctrine that wins the eternal victory in small things as in great."

"I say, Granpa, did you ever read any books by Charmian Piper?"

"Oh rather, we all knew her books. She was a fine-looking woman. You should have heard her read poetry from a platform in the days of Poetry. Harold Munro always said—"

"Her son, Eric, has told me there's talk of her novels being reprinted. There's a revival of interest in her novels. There's been an article written, Eric says. But he says the novels all consist of people saying 'touché' to each other, and it's all an affectation, the revival of interest, just because his mother is so old and still alive and was famous once."

"She's still famous. Always has been. Your trouble is, you know nothing, Olive. Everyone knows Charmian Piper."

"Oh no they don't. No one's heard of her except a few old people, but there's going to be a revival. I say there's been an article—"

"You know nothing about literature."

"Touché" she snapped, for Percy himself was always pretending that nobody had forgotten his poetry, really. Then she gave him three pounds to make up for her cruelty, which in fact he had not noticed; he simply did not acknowledge the idea of revival in either case, since he did not recognise the interim death. However, he took the three pounds from Olive, of whose side-line activities he was unaware, for, besides having small private means from her mother's side, she also had occasional jobs as an actress on the B.B.C.

He carried the money by bus and underground to Leicester Square where the post office was open all night, and wrote out, on several telegraph forms, in large slow capitals, a wire to Guy Leet, The Old Stable, Stedrost, Surrey: "You are fantastically wrong in your reference to Ernest Dowson that exceedingly poignant poet who only just steered clear of sentimentality and self-pity stop Ernest Dowson was the spiritual and aesthetic child of Swinburne Tennyson and especially Verlaine by whose verse he was veritably haunted Dowsons verse requires to be read aloud which is more than most verse by later hands can stand up to stop I cried for madder music and for stronger wine new line but when the feast is finished and the lamps expire new line then falls thy shadow. Cynara the night is thine new line and I am desolate and sick of an old passion etcetera stop read it aloud man your cheap alliterative jibe carries no weight you are fantastically wrong—Percy Mannering."

He handed in the sheaf of forms at the counter. The clerk looked closely at Percy, whereupon Percy made visible the three pound notes.

"Are you sure," said the clerk then, "you want to send all this?"

"I am," bawled Percy Mannering. He handed over two of the notes, took his change and went out into the bright-lit night.

Chapter Eight

Dame Lettie Colston had been happier without a resident maid, but the telephone incidents had now forced on her the necessity of having someone in the house to answer the dreadful calls. The mystery of it was, that the man never gave the terrible message to the girl. On the other hand, in the two weeks since her arrival, there had been a series of calls which proved to be someone getting the wrong number. When they had occurred three times in one day Dame Lettie began to bewilder the girl with questions.

"Who was it, Gwen, was it a man?"

"It was a wrong number."

"Was it a man?"

"Yes, but it was a wrong number."

"What did he say exactly? Do answer my question please."

"He said, 'Sorry, it's a wrong number,'" shouted Gwen, "that's what he said."

"What kind of voice was it?"

"Oh mad-um. I said it was a man, didn't I? The lines must be crossed. I know phones like the back of my hand."

"Yes, but was the voice young or old? Was it the same one as got the last wrong number?"

"Well, they're all the same to me, if they're wrong numbers. You better answer the phone yourself and then—"

"I was only asking," said Dame Lettie, "because we

seem to be having such a lot of wrong numbers since you've been here. And it always seems to be a man."

"What you mean? What exactly you mean by that, mad-*um?*"

Dame Lettie had not meant whatever the girl thought she meant. It was Gwen's evening out, and Lettie was glad Godfrey was coming to dine with her.

At about eight o'clock, when they were at dinner, the telephone rang.

"Godfrey, you answer it please."

He marched out into the hall. She heard him lift the receiver and give the number. "Yes, that's right," he said next. "Who's that, who is it?" Lettie heard him say. Then he replaced the receiver.

"Godfrey," she said, "that was the man?"

"Yes," he shouted. " 'Tell Dame Lettie to remember she must die.' Then he rang off. Damned peculiar." He sat down and continued eating his soup.

"There is no need to shout, Godfrey. Keep calm." Her own large body was trembling.

"Well, it's damned odd. I say you must have an enemy. Sounds a common little fellow, with his lisp."

"Oh no, Godfrey, he is quite cultured. But sinister."

"I say he's a common chap. This isn't the first time I've heard him."

"There must be something wrong with your hearing, Godfrey. A middle-aged, cultivated man who should know better—"

"A barrow boy, I should say."

"Nonsense. Go and ring the police. They said always to report—"

"What's the use?" he said. And seeing she would argue, he added, "After dinner. I'll ring after dinner."

"That is the first time he has left that message since I took on Gwen a fortnight ago. When Gwen answers the telephone the man says, 'Sorry, wrong number.' He does it two or three times a day."

"It may *be* some fellow getting a wrong number. Your lines must be crossed with someone else's. Have you reported this nuisance to the Exchange?"

"I have," she said. "They tell me the lines are perfectly in order."

"They must be crossed—"

"Oh," she said, "you are as bad as Gwen, going on about crossed lines. I have a good idea who it is. I think it is Chief Inspector Mortimer."

"Nothing like Mortimer's voice."

"Or his accomplice," she said.

"Rubbish. A man in his position."

"That is why the police don't find the culprit. They know, but they won't reveal his identity. He is their former Chief."

"I say you have an enemy."

"I say it is Mortimer."

"Why, then," said Godfrey, "do you continue to consult him about the case?"

"So that he shall not know I suspect him. He may then fall into a trap. Meantime, as I have told you, he is out of my will. He doesn't know *that.*"

"Oh, you are always changing your will. No wonder you have enemies." Godfrey felt guilty at having gossiped to Olive about Lettie's changes in her will. "No wonder," he said, "you don't know the culprit."

"I haven't heard from Eric lately," Dame Lettie remarked, so that he felt more guilty, thinking of all he had told Olive.

Godfrey said, "He has been in London the past six weeks. He returned to Cornwall last night."

"But he hasn't been to see me. Why didn't you let me know before, Godfrey?"

"I myself did not know he was in London," said Godfrey, "until I learned it from a mutual friend yesterday."

"What mutual friend? What has Eric been up to? What friend?"

"I cannot recollect at the moment," said Godfrey. "I have long given up interest in Eric's affairs."

"You should keep your memory in training," she said. "Try going over in your mind each night before retiring everything you have done during the day. I must say I am astonished that Eric did not call upon me."

"He didn't come near us," said Godfrey, "so why should he come to see you?"

"At least," she said, "I should have thought he knew what side his bread's buttered."

"Ha, you don't know Eric. Fifty-six years of age and an utter failure. You ought to know, Lettie, that men of that age and type can't bear the sight of old people. It reminds them that they are getting on. Ha, and he's feeling his age, I hear. You, Lettie, may yet see him under. We may both see him under."

Lying in bed later that night, it seemed clear to Dame Lettie that Eric must really after all be the man behind the telephone calls. He would not ring himself lest she should recognise his voice. He must have an accomplice. She rose and switched on the light.

Dame Lettie sat in her dressing gown at dead of night and re-filled her fountain pen. While she did so she glanced at the page she had just written. She thought, How shaky my writing looks! Immediately, as if slamming a door on it, she put the thought out of sight. She wiped the nib of her pen, turned over the sheet and continued, on the back, her letter to Eric:

. . . and so, having heard of your having been in London these past six weeks, your not having informed me, far less called, does, I admit, strike me as being, to say the least, discourteous. I had wished to consult you on certain matters relating to your Mother. There is every indication that we shall have to arrange for her to be sent to the nursing home in Surrey of which I told you when last I saw you.

She laid down her pen, withdrew one of the fine hairpins from her thin hair, and replaced it. Perhaps, she thought, I should take an even more subtle line with Eric. Her face puckered in folds under the desk-lamp. Two thoughts intruded simultaneously. One was: I am really very tired; and the other: I am not a bit tired, I am charging ahead with great energy. She lifted the pen again and continued to put the wavering marks across the page.

I have recently been making some slight adjustments in my own affairs, about which I could have wished to consult you had you seen fit to inform me of your recent visit to London.

Was that subtle enough? No, it was too subtle, perhaps, for Eric.

These *minor* adjustments, of course, have some bearing upon my Will. It has always seemed to me a pity that your cousin Martin, though doing so well in South Africa, should not be remembered in some small way. I would wish for no recriminations among the family after my passing. Your position is of course substantially unchanged, but I could wish you had made yourself available for consultation. You will recall the adjustments I made to existing arrangements after your cousin Alan fell on the field of battle. . . .

That is good, she thought, that is subtle. Eric had got out of the war somehow. She continued,

I could have wished for discussions with you, but I am an old woman and quite realise that you, who are nearing the end of your prime, must be full of affairs. Mr. Merrilees is now drawing up the amended Will and I would not wish to further interfere with existing arrangements. Nevertheless, I could have wished to discuss them with you had you seen fit to present yourself during the six weeks of your recent stay in London, of which I did not hear until after your return.

That ought to do it, she thought. He will come wheezing down from Cornwall as fast as the first train will carry him. If he is the guilty man he will know that I *know*. No one, she thought, is going to kill me through fear. And she fell to wondering again, who her enemy could be. She fell to doubting whether Eric had it in him . . . whether he had the financial means to employ an accomplice. Easier, she thought, for Mortimer. Anyway, she thought, it must be someone who is in my Will. And so she sealed and stamped her letter to Eric, placed it on the tray in the hall, took a tot of whisky and went to bed. Her head moved slowly from side to side on the pillow, for she could not sleep. She had caught a chill down there in the study. A cramp seized her leg. She had a longing for a strong friend, some major Strength from which to draw. Who can help me? she thought. Godfrey is selfish, Charmian feeble, Jean Taylor is bedridden. I can talk to Taylor, but she has not got the strength I need. Alec Warner . . . shall I go to see Alec Warner? I never got strength from him. Neither did Taylor. He has not got the strength one needs.

Suddenly she sprang up. Something had lightly touched her cheek. She switched on the light. A spider on her pillow, large as a penny, quite still, with its brown legs outspread! She looked at it feverishly then pulled herself together to try to pick it off the pillow. As she put forth her hand another, paler, spider-legged and fluffy creature on the pillow where the bed-lamp cast a shade, caught her sight. "Gwen!" she screams. "Gwen!"

But Gwen is sleeping soundly. In a panic Dame Lettie

plucks at the large spider. It proves to be a feather. So does the other object

She dropped her head on her pillow once more. She thought: My old pillows, I shall get some new pillows.

She put out the light and the troubled movements of the head began again. Whom, she thought, can I draw Strength from? She considered her acquaintances one by one—who among them was tougher, stronger than she?

Tempest, she thought at last. I shall get Tempest Sidebottome to help me. Tempest, her opponent in forty years' committee-sitting, had frequently been a painful idea to Dame Lettie. Particularly had she resented Tempest's bossy activeness and physical agility at Lisa's funeral. Strangely, now, she drew strength from the thought of the woman. Tempest Sidebottome would settle the matter if anyone could. Tempest would hunt down the persecutor. Dame Lettie's head settled still on the pillow. She would go over to Richmond tomorrow and talk to Tempest. After all, Tempest was only seventy. She hoped her idiotic husband Ronald would be out. But in any case, he was deaf. Dame Lettie turned at last to her sleep, deriving a half-dreamt success from the strength of Tempest Sidebottome as from some tremendous mother.

"Good morning, Eric," said Charmian as she worked her way round the breakfast table to her place.

"*Not* Eric," said Mrs. Pettigrew. "We are a bit confused again this morning."

"Are you, my dear. What has happened to confuse you?" said Charmian.

Godfrey sensed the start of bickering, so he looked up from his paper and said to his wife, "Lettie was telling me last night that it is a great aid to memory to go through in one's mind each night the things which have happened in the course of the day."

"Why," said Charmian, "that is a Catholic practice.

We are always recommended to consider each night our actions of the past day. It is an admirable—"

"Not the same thing," said Godfrey, "at all. You are speaking exclusively of one's moral actions. What I'm talking about are things which have happened. It is a great aid to memory, as Lettie was saying last night, to memorise everything which has occurred in one's experience during the day. Your practice, which you call Catholic, is, moreover, common to most religions. To my mind, that type of examination of conscience is designed to enslave the individual and inhibit his freedom of action. Take yourself, for example. You only have to appeal to psychology—"

"To whom?" said Charmian cattily, as she took the cup which Mrs. Pettigrew passed to her.

Godfrey turned back to his paper. Whereupon Charmian continued the argument with Mrs. Pettigrew.

"I don't see that one can examine one's moral conduct without memorising everything that's happened during the day. It is the same thing. What Lettie advises is a form of—"

Godfrey put down his paper. "I say it is not the same thing." He dipped an oblong of toast in his tea and put it in his mouth.

Mrs. Pettigrew rose to the opportunity of playing the peacemaker. "Now hush," she said to Charmian. "Eat your nice scrambled egg which Taylor has prepared for you."

"Taylor is not here," stated Charmian.

"Taylor—what do you mean?" said Godfrey.

Mrs. Pettigrew winked at him.

Godfrey opened his mouth to retort, then shut it again.

"Taylor is in hospital," said Charmian, pleased with her clarity.

Godfrey read from the newspaper, " 'Motling—' are you listening, Charmian?—'on 10th December at Zomba, Nyasaland; Major Cosmos Petwick Motling, G.C.V.O., husband of the late Eugenie, beloved father of Patricia and Eugen, in his 91st year.' Are you listening, Charmian?"

"Was he killed at the front, dear?"

"Ah, me!" said Mrs. Pettigrew.

Godfrey opened his mouth to say something to Mrs. Pettigrew, then stopped. He held up the paper again and from behind it mumbled, "No, Zomba. Motling's the name. He went out there to retire. You won't remember him."

"*I* recall him well," said Mrs. Pettigrew; "when his wife was alive, Lisa used to—"

"Was he killed at the front?" said Charmian.

"The front," said Mrs. Pettigrew.

" 'Sidebottome,' " said Godfrey, "are you listening, Charmian?— 'On 18th December at the Mandeville Nursing Home, Richmond; Tempest Ethel, beloved wife of Ronald Charles Sidebottome. Funeral private.' Doesn't give her age."

"Tempest Sidebottome!" said Mrs. Pettigrew, reaching to take the paper from his hand. "Let me see."

Godfrey withdrew the paper and opened his mouth as if to protest, then closed it again. However, he said, "I am not finished with the paper."

"Well, fancy Tempest Sidebottome," said Mrs. Pettigrew. "Of course, cancer is cancer."

"She always *was* a bitch," said Godfrey, as if her death were the ultimate proof of it.

"I wonder," said Mrs. Pettigrew, "who will look after poor old Ronald now. He's so deaf."

Godfrey looked at her to see more closely what she meant, but her short broad nose was hidden by her cup and her eyes stared appraisingly at the marmalade.

She was, in fact, quite shocked by Tempest's death. She had only a month ago agreed to join forces with the Sidebottomes in contesting Lisa Brooke's will. Tempest, when she had learnt of Guy Leet's hitherto secret marriage to Lisa, had been driven to approach Mrs. Pettigrew and attempt to make up their recent differences. Mrs. Pettigrew had rather have worked alone, but the heavy costs deterred her. She had agreed to go in with Tempest against Guy Leet on the grounds that his marriage with Lisa Brooke had not been consummated. They had been warned that their case was a slender one, but Tempest had the money and the drive to go ahead, and Mrs. Pettigrew had in her possession the relevant correspondence. Ronald Sidebottome had been timid about the affair—didn't like raking up the scandal, but Tempest had seemed to have the drive. Tempest's death was a shock to Mrs. Pettigrew. She would have to work hard on Ronald. One got no rest. She stared at the marmalade pot as if to fathom its possibilities.

Godfrey had returned to his paper. "Funeral private. That saves us a wreath."

"You had better write to poor Ronald," said Charmian, "and I will say a rosary for Tempest. Oh, I do remember her as a girl. She was newly out from Australia and her uncle was a rector in Dorset—as was also my uncle, Mrs. Pettigrew—"

"Your uncle was not in Dorset. He was up in Yorkshire," said Godfrey.

"But he was a country rector, like Tempest's uncle. Leave me alone, Godfrey. I am just telling Mrs. Pettigrew."

"Oh, do call me Mabel," said Mrs. Pettigrew, winking at Godfrey.

"Her uncle, Mabel," said Charmian, "was a rector and so was mine. It was the thing we had in common. We had not a great deal in common, Mrs. Pettigrew, and of course as a girl she was considerably younger than me."

"She is still younger than you," said Godfrey.

"No, Godfrey, not now. Well, Mrs. Pettigrew, I do so

remember our two uncles together and we were all staying down in Dorset. There was a bishop and a dean, and our two uncles. Oh, poor Tempest was bored. They were discussing the Scriptures and this manuscript called 'Q.' How Tempest was in a rage when she heard that 'Q' was only a manuscript, because she had imagined them to be talking of a bishop and she said out loud '*Who* is Bishop Kew?' And of course everyone laughed heartily, and then they were sorry for Tempest. And they tried to console her by telling her that 'Q' was nothing really, not even a manuscript, which indeed it wasn't, and I must confess I never understood how they could sit up so late at night fitting their ideas into this 'Q' which is nothing really. As I say poor Tempest was in a rage, she could never bear to be made game of."

Mrs. Pettigrew winked at Godfrey.

"Charmian," said Godfrey, "you are over-exciting yourself." And true enough, she was tremulously crying.

Chapter Nine

Partly because of a reorganisation of the Maud Long Ward and partly because of Tempest Sidebottome's death, Sister Burstead was transferred to another ward.

She had been a protégée of Tempest's, and this had mostly accounted for the management committee's resistance to any previous suggestion that the sister could not cope with the old people's ward. The committee, though largely composed of recently empowered professional men and women, had been in many ways afraid of Tempest. Or rather, afraid to lose her lest they should get someone worse.

It was necessary for them to tolerate at least one or two remnants of the old-type committee people until they should die out. And they chiefly feared, in fact, that if Tempest should take offence and resign, she would be replaced by some more formidable, more subtle private welfare-worker and busybody. And whereas Tempest had many dramatic things to say in committee, whereas she was imperious with the matron, an opponent on principle of all occasions of expenditure, scornful in the extreme of physiotherapists and psychiatrists (everything beginning "psycho-" or "physio-" Tempest lumped together, believed to be the same thing, and dismissed)—although she was in reaction against the committee's ideals, she was so to the point of parody, and it was for precisely this reason, because she so much demonstrated the errors of her system, that she was retained, was propitiated from time to time, and allowed to have her way in such minor matters as that of Sister Burstead. Not that the committee were not afraid of Tempest for other, less evident reasons; but these were matters of instinct and not openly admitted. Her voice in committee had been strangely terrifying to many an eminent though small-boned specialist, even the bossy young heavily-qualified women had sometimes failed to outstare the little pale pebble-eyes of the great unself-questioning matriarch, Mrs. Sidebottome. "Terrible woman," everyone always agreed when she had left.

"After the fifties are over," said the chairman who was himself a man of seventy-three, "everything will be easier. This transition period . . . the old brigade don't like change. They don't like loss of authority. By the middle-sixties everything will be easier. We will have things in working order." Whereupon the committee surrendered themselves to putting up with Tempest, a rock of unchanging, until the middle-sixties of the century should arrive, leaving behind her on the committee a Tempest-shaped vacuum which they immediately attempted, but had not yet been able to fill.

In the meantime, as if tempting Providence to send them another Tempest, they transferred Sister Burstead, on the first of January, to another ward. That the old people's ward was being reorganised provided a reasonable excuse, and Sister Burstead made no further protest.

News of the transfer reached the grannies before the news of the reorganisation.

"I'll believe it when I see it," said Granny Barnacle.

She saw it before that week-end. A new ward sister, fat and forceful with a huge untroubled faceful of flesh and brisk legs, was installed. "That's how I like them," said Granny Barnacle. "Sister Bastard was too skinny."

The new sister, when she caught Granny Green absent-mindedly scooping the scrambled egg off her plate into her locker, put her hands on her slab-like hips and said, "What the hell do you think you're doing?"

"That's how I like them," said Granny Barnacle. She closed her eyes on her pillow with contentment. She declared herself to feel safe for the first time for months. She declared herself ready to die now that she had seen the removal of Sister Bastard. She sprang up again from her pillow and with outstretched arm and pointing finger prophesied that the whole ward would now see the winter through.

Miss Valvona, who was always much affected by Miss Barnacle's feelings, consulted the stars: "Granny Barnacle —*Sagittarius*. 'Noon period best for commencing long-distance travel. You can show your originality to-day.'"

"Ho!" said Granny Barnacle. "Originality to-day, I'll wear me britches back to front."

The nurses came on their daily round of washing, changing, combing and prettifying the patients before the matron's inspection. They observed Granny Barnacle's excitement and decided to leave her to the last. She was usually excitable throughout this performance in any case. During Sister Burstead's term of office, especially, Granny Barnacle would screech when turned over for her back to be dusted with powder, or helped out of bed to sit on her chair.

"Nurse, I'll be covered with bruises," she would shout.

"If you don't move, Gran, you'll be covered with bedsores."

She would scream to God that the nurses were pulling her arms from their sockets, she would swear by the Almighty that she wasn't fit to be sat up. She moaned, whenever the physiotherapist made her move her fingers and toes, and declared that her joints would crack.

"Kill me off," she would command, "and be done with it."

"Come on, Gran, you've got to get exercise."

"Crack! Can't you hear the bones crack? Kill me off and—"

"Let's rub your legs, Gran. My, you've got beautiful legs."

"Help, she's killing me."

But at the best of times Granny Barnacle really liked an excuse for a bit of noise, it livened her up. In a sense, she gave vent to the whole ward's will to shout, so that the others did not make nearly so much noise as they might otherwise have done. It was true some of the other grannies were loud in complaints, but this was mostly for a few seconds when their hair was being combed. Granny Green would never fail to tell the nurses after her hair was done:

"I had a lovely head of hair till you cut it off," although in reality there had been very little to cut off.

"It's hygiene, Granny. It would hurt far more when we combed it if your hair was long."

"I had a lovely head. . . ."

"Me, too," Granny Barnacle would declare, especially if Sister Burstead had been within hearing. "You should have seen my head before they cut it off."

"Oh, short hair is cooler when one is in bed," Granny Taylor, whose hair had really been long and thick, and who actually preferred it short, would murmur to herself.

"Let's give you a nice wave to-day, Granny Barnacle."

"Oh, you're killing me."

On the day of the new sister's arrival, Granny Barnacle and her obvious excitement having been left to the last, it was found, when her turn came, that she was running a temperature.

"Get me out of bed, love," she implored the nurse. "Let's sit up to-day, seeing Bastard's gone."

"No, you've got a temperature."

"Nurse, I want to get up to-day. Get me a will-form,

※ 114 ※

there's a bob in my locker, I want to make a new will and put in the new sister. What's her name?"

"Lucy."

"Lucy Locket," shrieked Granny Barnacle, "lost her—"

"Lie still, Granny Barnacle, till we make you better."

She submitted after a fuss. Next day, when they told her she must keep her bed she protested louder, even struggled a little, but Miss Taylor in the opposite bed noticed that Granny Barnacle's voice was unusually thin and high.

"Nurse, I'm going to get up to-day. Get me a will-form. I want to make a new will and put in the new sister. What's her name?"

"Lucy," said the nurse. "Your blood pressure's high, Gran."

"Her last name, girl."

"Lucy. Sister Lucy."

"Sister Lousy," screamed Granny Barnacle. "Well, she's going in my will. Give me a hand. . . ."

When the doctor had gone she was given an injection and dozed off for a while.

At one o'clock, while everyone else was eating, she woke. Sister Lucy brought some milk custard to her bed and fed her with a spoon. The ward was quiet and the sound of grannies' spoons tinkling on their plates became more pronounced in the absence of voices.

About three o'clock Granny Barnacle woke again and started to rave in a piping voice, at first faintly, then growing higher and piercing. "Noos, E'ning Noos," fluted the old newsvendor. "E'ning pap-*ar*, Noos, E'ning Stan-*ar*, E'ning Stah Noos *an* Stan-*ar*."

She was given an injection and a sip of water. Her bed was wheeled to the end of the ward and a screen was put round it. In the course of the afternoon the doctor came, stayed behind the screen for a short while, and went.

The new ward sister came and looked behind the screen

from time to time. Towards five o'clock, when the few visitors were going home, Sister Lucy went behind the screen once more. She spoke to Granny Barnacle, who replied in a weak voice.

"She's conscious," said Miss Valvona.

"Yes, she spoke."

"Is she bad?" said Miss Valvona as the sister passed her bed.

"She's not too well," said the sister.

Some of the patients kept looking expectantly and fearfully at the entrance to the ward, whenever anyone was heard approaching, as if watching for the Angel of Death. Towards six o'clock came the sound of a man's footsteps. The patients, propped up with their supper trays, stopped eating and turned to see who had arrived.

Sure enough, it was the priest, carrying a small box. Miss Valvona and Miss Taylor crossed themselves as he passed. He went behind the screen accompanied by a nurse. Though the ward was silent, none of the patients had sharp enough ears, even with their hearing-aids, to catch more than an occasional humming sound from his recitations.

Miss Valvona's tears dropped into her supper. She was thinking of her father's Last Sacrament, after which he had recovered to live a further six months. The priest behind the screen would be committing Granny Barnacle to the sweet Lord, he would be anointing Granny Barnacle's eyes, nose, mouth, hands and feet, asking pardon for the sins she had committed by sight, by hearing, smell, taste and speech, by the touch of her hands, and by her very footsteps.

The priest left. A few of the patients finished their supper. Those who did not were coaxed with Ovaltine. At seven the sister took a last look behind the screen before going off to the dining-room.

"How is she now?" said a granny.

"Sleeping nicely."

About twenty minutes later a nurse looked behind the screen, went inside for a moment, then came out again. The patients watched her leave the ward. There she gave her message to the runner who went to the dining-room and, opening the door, caught the attention of the ward sister. The runner lifted up one finger to signify that one of the sister's patients had died.

It was the third death in the ward since Miss Taylor's admittance. She knew the routine. "We leave the patient for an hour in respect for the dead," a nurse had once explained to her, "but no longer than an hour, because the body begins to set. Then we perform the last offices—that's washing them and making them right for burial."

At five past nine, by the dim night-lamps of the ward, Granny Barnacle was wheeled away.

"I shan't sleep a wink," said Mrs. Reewes-Duncan. Many said they would not sleep a wink, but in fact they slept more soundly and exhaustedly that night than on most nights. The ward lay till morning still and sound-less, breathing like one body instead of eleven.

The reorganisation of the Maud Long Ward began next day, and all patients declared it a mercy for Granny Barnacle that she had been spared it.

Hitherto, the twelve beds in the Maud Long Ward had occupied only half of the space in the room; they had been a surplus from another, larger, medical ward, comprised mainly of elderly women. The new arrangement was designed to fill up the remaining half of the Maud Long Ward with a further nine elderly patients. These were to be put at the far end. Already, while the preparations were still in progress, this end of the ward was referred to among the nurses as the "geriatric corner."

"What's that word mean they keep saying?" Granny Roberts demanded of Miss Taylor.

"It's to do with old age. There must be some very old patients coming in."

"We supposed to be teen-agers, then?"

Granny Valvona said, "Our new friends will probably be centenarians."

"I didn't catch—just a minute till I get the trumpet right," said Granny Roberts, who always referred to her small hearing fixture as the trumpet.

"See," said Granny Green, "what they're bringing in to the ward."

A line of cots was being wheeled up the ward and arranged in the new geriatric corner. These cots were much the same as the other hospital beds, but with the startling difference that they had high railed sides like children's cots.

Granny Valvona crossed herself.

Next, the patients were wheeled in. Perhaps this was not the best introduction of the newcomers to the old established set. Being in varying advanced states of senility, and also being specially upset by the move, the new arrivals were making more noise and dribbling more from the mouth than usual.

Sister Lucy came round the grannies' beds, explaining that they would have to be patient with these advanced cases. Knitting needles must not be left lying about near the geriatric corner, in case any of the newcomers should hurt themselves. The patients were not to be alarmed if anything *funny* should occur. At this point the sister had to call a nurse's attention to one of the new patients, a frail, wizened, but rather pretty little woman, who was trying to climb over the side of her cot. The nurse rushed to settle the old woman back in bed. The patient set up an infant-like wail, yet not entirely that of a child—it was more like that of an old woman copying the cry of an infant.

The sister continued addressing the grannies in confidential tones. "You must try to remember," she said, "that these cases are very advanced, poor dears. And don't get upset, like good girls. Try and help the nurses by keeping quiet and tidy."

"We'll soon be senile ourselves at this rate," said Granny Green.

"Sh-sh," said the sister. "We don't use that word. They are geriatric cases."

When she had gone Granny Duncan said, "To think that I spent my middle years looking forward to my old age and a rest!"

Another geriatric case was trying to climb over the cot. A nurse bustled to the rescue.

"A mercy," said Granny Duncan, "poor Granny Barnacle didn't live to see it. Poor souls— Don't you be rough with her, Nurse!"

The patient had, in fact, pulled the nurse's cap off and was now clamouring for a drink of water. The nurse replaced her cap, and while another nurse held a plastic beaker of water to the old woman's lips, assured the ward, "They'll settle down. The moving's upset them."

After a stormy night, the newcomers did seem quieter next morning, though one or two made a clamour in the ordinary course of conversation, and most, when they were helped out of bed to stand shakily upheld for a moment by the nurse, wet the floor. In the afternoon a specialist lady and an assistant came with draught-boards which she laid on the floor beside four of the new patients who were sitting up in chairs, but whose hands were crippled. They did not protest when their socks and slippers were removed and their feet manipulated and rubbed by the younger woman. Their socks and slippers were replaced and they seemed to know what to do when the draught-boards were set in front of their feet.

"Look, did you ever," said Granny Valvona. "They're playing draughts with their feet."

"I ask you," said Granny Roberts, "is it a bloody circus we are here?"

"That's nothing to what you'll see in Geriatrics," said the nurse proudly.

"A blessing poor Granny Barnacle wasn't spared to see it."

Miss Taylor absorbed as much of the new experience as she could, for the sake of Alec Warner. But the death of Granny Barnacle, her own arthritic pains, and the noisy intrusion of the senile cases, had confused her. She was crying towards the end of the day, and worried lest the nurse should catch her at it, and perhaps report her too sick to be wheeled down next morning to the Mass which she and Miss Valvona had requested for the soul of Granny Barnacle who had no relatives to mourn her.

Miss Taylor dropped asleep, and waking in the middle of the night because of her painful limbs, still pretended to sleep on, and went without her injection. At eleven o'clock next morning Miss Valvona and Miss Taylor were wheeled into the hospital chapel. They were accompanied by three other grannies, not Catholics, from the Maud Long Ward who had been attached to Granny Barnacle in various ways, including those of love, scorn, resentment and pity.

During the course of the Mass an irrational idea streaked through Miss Taylor's mind. She dismissed it and concentrated on her prayers. But this irrational idea, which related to the identity of Dame Lettie's tormentor, was to return to her later again and again.

Chapter Ten

"Is that Mr. Godfrey Colston?" said the man on the telephone.

"Yes, speaking."

"Remember you must die," said the man.

"Dame Lettie is not here," he said, being flustered. "Who is that speaking?"

"The message is for you, Mr. Colston."

"Who is speaking?"

The man had hung up.

Though Godfrey was still tall, he had seemed to shrink during the winter, to an extent that an actual tape-measure would perhaps not confirm. His bones were larger than ever; that is to say, they remained the same size as they had been throughout his adult life, but the ligaments between them had gradually shrunk, as they do with advancing age, so that the bones appeared huge-grown. This process had, in Godfrey, increased rapidly in the months between the autumn of Mrs. Pettigrew's joining his household and the March morning when he received the telephone call.

He put down the receiver and walked with short steps into the library. Mrs. Pettigrew followed him. She herself was looking healthier and not much older.

"Who was that on the phone, Godfrey?" she said.

"A man . . . I can't understand. It should have been

for Lettie but he definitely said it was for me. I thought the message—"

"What did he say?"

"That thing he says to Lettie. But he said 'Mr. Colston, it's for you, Mr. Colston.' I don't understand. . . ."

"Look here," said Mrs. Pettigrew, "let's pull ourselves together, shall we?"

"Have you got the key of the sideboard on you?"

"I have," said Mabel Pettigrew. "Want a drink?"

"I feel I need a little—"

"I'll bring one in to you. Sit down."

"A stiff one."

"Sit down. There's a boy."

She came back, spritely in her black dress and the new white-streaked lock of hair among the very black, sweeping from her brow. Her hair had been cut shorter. She had painted her nails pink and wore two large rings which gave an appearance of opulent ancient majesty to the long wrinkled hand which held Godfrey's glass of brandy and soda.

"Thanks," said Godfrey, taking the glass. "Many thanks." He sat back and drank his brandy, looking at her from time to time as if to see what she was going to do and say.

She sat opposite him. She said nothing till he had finished. Then she said, "Now, look."

She said, "Now, look. This is all imagination."

He muttered something about being in charge of his faculties.

"In that case," she said—"in *that* case, have you seen your lawyer yet?"

He muttered something about next week.

"You have an appointment with him," she said, "this afternoon."

"This afternoon? Who—how . . . ?"

"I've made an appointment for you to see him at three this afternoon."

"Not this afternoon," said Godfrey. "Don't feel up to it. Draughty office. Next week."

"You can take a taxi if you don't feel up to driving. It's no distance."

"Next week," he shouted, for the brandy had restored him.

However, the effects wore off. At lunch Charmian said, "Is there anything the matter, Godfrey?"

The telephone rang. Godfrey looked up, startled. He said to Mrs. Pettigrew, "Don't answer."

Mrs. Pettigrew merely said, "I wonder if Mrs. Anthony has heard it? I bet she hasn't."

Mrs. Anthony's hearing was beginning to fail, and she had obviously not heard the telephone.

Mrs. Pettigrew strode out into the hall and lifted the receiver. She came back presently and addressed Charmian.

"For you," she said. "The photographer wants to come to-morrow at four."

"Very well," said Charmian.

"I shan't be here, you know, to-morrow afternoon."

"That's all right," said Charmian. "He does not wish to photograph *you*. Say that four o'clock will be splendid."

While Mrs. Pettigrew went to give the message, Godfrey said, "Another reporter?"

"No, a photographer."

"I don't like the idea of all these strangers coming to the house. I had a nasty experience this morning. Put him off." He rose from his seat and shouted through the door, "I say, Mrs. Pettigrew, we don't want him coming here. Put him off, will you?"

"Too late," said Mrs. Pettigrew, resuming her place.

Mrs. Anthony looked round the door.

"Was you wanting something?"

"We did hope," said Mrs. Pettigrew very loudly, "to have our meal without interruptions. However, I have answered the telephone."

"Very good of you, I'm sure," said Mrs. Anthony, and disappeared.

Godfrey was still protesting about the photographer. "We'll have to put him off. Too many strangers."

Charmian said, "I shall not be here long, Godfrey."

"Come, come," said Mrs. Pettigrew. "You may well last another ten years."

"Quite," said Charmian, "and so I have decided to go away to the nursing home in Surrey, after all. I understand the arrangements there are almost perfect. One has every privacy. Oh, how one comes to appreciate privacy."

Mrs. Pettigrew lit a cigarette and slowly blew the smoke in Charmian's face.

"No one's interfering with your privacy," Godfrey muttered.

"And freedom," said Charmian. "I shall have freedom at the nursing home to entertain whom I please. Photographers, strangers—"

"There is no need," said Godfrey desperately, "for you to go away to a home now that you are so much improved."

Mrs. Pettigrew blew more smoke in Charmian's direction.

"Besides," he said, glancing at Mrs. Pettigrew, "we can't afford it."

Charmian was silent, as one who need not reply. Indeed, her books were bringing in money, and her small capital at least was safe from Mrs. Pettigrew. The revival of her novels during the past winter had sharpened her brain. Her memory had improved, and her physical health was better than it had been for years in spite of that attack of bronchitis in January, when a day and a night nurse had been in attendance for a week. However, she still had to move slowly and was prone to kidney trouble.

She looked at Godfrey who was wolfing his rice pudding without, she was sure, noticing what he was eating, and she wondered what was on his mind. She wondered what new torment Mrs. Pettigrew was practising upon him. She wondered how much of his past life Mrs. Pettigrew had discovered, and why he felt is necessary to hush it up at all such costs. She wondered where her own duty to Godfrey lay—where does one's duty as a wife reach its limits? She longed to be away in the nursing home in Surrey, and was surprised at this longing of hers, since all her life she had suffered from apprehensions of being in the power of strangers, and Godfrey had always seemed better than the devil she did not know.

"To move from your home at the age of eighty-seven," Godfrey was saying in an almost pleading voice, "might kill you. There is no need."

Mrs. Pettigrew, having pressed the bell in vain, said, "Oh, Mrs. Anthony is quite deaf. She must get an aid," and went to tell Mrs. Anthony to fetch her tea and Charmian's milk.

When she had gone, Godfrey said,

"I had an unpleasant experience this morning."

Charmian took refuge in a vague expression. She was terrified lest Godfrey was about to make some embarrassing confession concerning Mrs. Pettigrew.

"Are you listening, Charmian?" said Godfrey.

"Yes, oh yes. Anything you like."

"There was a telephone call from Lettie's man."

"Poor Lettie, I wonder he isn't tired of tormenting her."

"The call was for me. He said, 'The message is for you, Mr. Colston.' I am not imagining anything, mind you. I heard it with my ears."

"Really? What message?"

"You *know* what message," he said.

"Well, I should treat it as it deserves to be treated."

"What do you mean?"

"Neither more nor less," said Charmian.

"I'd like to know who the fellow is. I'd like to know why the police haven't got him. It's preposterous when we pay our rates and taxes to be threatened like that by a stranger."

"What did he threaten to do?" said Charmian. "I thought he merely always said—"

"It's upsetting," said Godfrey. "One might easily take a stroke in consequence. If it occurs again I shall write to *The Times*."

"Why not consult Mrs. Pettigrew," said Charmian. "She is a tower of strength."

Then she felt suddenly sorry for him, huddled among his bones. She left him and climbed the stairs slowly, clinging to the banister, to take her afternoon rest. She considered whether she could bring herself to leave Godfrey in his plight with Mrs. Pettigrew. After all, she herself might have been in an awkward situation, if she had not taken care, long before her old age, to destroy all possibly embarrassing documents. She smiled as she looked at her little bureau with its secretive appearance, in which Mrs. Pettigrew had found no secret, although Charmian knew she had penetrated behind those locks. But Godfrey, after all, was not a clever man.

In the end Godfrey submitted, and agreed to keep the appointment with his lawyer. Mrs. Pettigrew would not absolutely have refused to let him put it off for another day, had she not been frightened by his report of the telephone call. Obviously, his mind was going funny. She had not looked for this. He had better see the lawyer before anyone could say he had been talked into anything.

He got out the car and drove off. About ten minutes later Mrs. Pettigrew got a taxi at the end of the street and followed him. She wanted just to make sure he was at the lawyer's, and she merely intended to drive past the offices to satisfy herself that Godfrey's car was outside.

His car was not outside. She made the driver take her round Sloane Square. There was still no sign of Godfrey's car. She got out and went into a café opposite the offices and sat where she could see him arrive. But by quarter to four there was still no sign of his car. It occurred to her that his memory had escaped him while on his way to the lawyer. He had sometimes remarked that his oculist and his chiropodist were in Chelsea. Perhaps he had gone, by mistake, to have his eyes tested or his feet done. She had trusted his faculties; he had always seemed all right until this morning; but after his silly talk this morning about that phone call anything could happen. It was to be remembered he was nearly eighty-eight.

Or was he cunning? Could the phone call have come from the lawyer, perhaps to confirm the appointment, and Godfrey have cancelled it? After all, how could he have suddenly gone crazy like his sister without showing preliminary signs? Possibly he had decided to feign feebleness of mind merely to evade his obligations.

Mrs. Pettigrew paid for her coffee, resumed her brown squirrel coat, and set off along the King's Road. She saw no sign of his car outside the chiropodist. Anyway, he had probably gone home. She glanced up a side turning and thought she saw Godfrey's car in the blue half-light parked outside a bombed building. Yes indeed, on investigation, it proved to be Godfrey's Vauxhall.

Mrs. Pettigrew looked expertly around her. The houses opposite the bombed building were all occupied and afforded no concealment. The bombed building itself seemed to demand investigation. She walked up the dusty steps on which strangely there stood a collection of grimy milk bottles. The broken door was partly open. She creaked it further open and looked inside. She could see right through, over the decayed brick and plaster, to the windows at the back of the house. She heard a noise as of rustling paper—or could it be rats? She stepped back and stood once more outside the door considering whether and how long she could bear to stand in that desolate doorway and see, without being seen, from which direction Godfrey should return to his car.

Charmian woke at four and sensed the emptiness of the house. Mrs. Anthony now went home at two in the afternoons. Both Godfrey and Mrs. Pettigrew must be out. Charmian lay listening, to confirm her feeling of being alone in the house. She heard no sound. She rose slowly, tidied herself and, groping for one after another banister rail, descended the stairs. She had reached the first half-landing when the telephone rang. She did not hurry, but it was still ringing when she reached it.

"Is that Mrs. Colston?"

"Yes, speaking."

"Charmian Piper—that's right, isn't it?"

"Yes. Are you a reporter?"

"Remember," he said, "you must die."

"Oh, as to that," she said, "for the past thirty years and more I have thought of it from time to time. My memory is failing in certain respects. I am gone eighty-six. But somehow I do not forget my death, whenever that will be."

"Delighted to hear it," he said. "Goodbye for now."

"Goodbye," she said. "What paper do you represent?"

But he had rung off.

Charmian made her way to the library and cautiously built up the fire which had burnt low. The effort of stooping tired her and she sat for a moment in the big chair. After a while it was tea-time. She thought, for a space, about tea. Then she made her way to the kitchen where the tray had been set by Mrs. Anthony in readiness for

Mrs. Pettigrew to make the tea. But Mrs. Pettigrew had gone out. Charmian felt overwhelmed suddenly with trepidation and pleasure. Could she make tea herself? Yes, she would try. The kettle was heavy as she held it under the tap. It was heavier still when it was half-filled with water. It rocked in her hand and her skinny, large-freckled wrist ached and wobbled with the strain. At last she had lifted the kettle safely on to the gas ring. She had seen Mrs. Anthony use the automatic lighter. She tried it but could not make it work. Matches. She looked everywhere for matches but could not find any. She went back to the library and took from a jar one of Godfrey's home-made tapers. She stooped dangerously and lit the taper at the fire. Then, cautiously, she bore the little quivering flame to the kitchen, holding it in one shaking hand, and holding that hand with her other hand to keep it as steady as possible. At last the gas was lit under the kettle. Charmian put the teapot on the stove to warm. She then sat down in Mrs. Anthony's chair to wait for the kettle to boil. She felt strong and fearless.

When the kettle had boiled she spooned tea into the pot and knew that the difficult part had come. She lifted the kettle a little and tilted its spout over the tea-pot. She stood as far back as she could. In went the hot water, and though it splashed quite a bit on the stove, she did not get any over her dress or her feet. She bore the tea-pot to the tray. It wafted to and fro, but she managed to place it down gently after all.

She looked at the hot-water jug. Should she bother with hot water? She had done so well up to now, it would be a pity to make any mistake and have an accident. But she felt strong and fearless. A pot of tea without the hot-water jug beside it was nonsense. She filled the jug, this time splashing her foot a little, but not enough to burn.

When all was set on the tray she was tempted to have her tea in the kitchen there in Mrs. Anthony's chair.

But she thought of her bright fire in the library. She looked at the tray. Plainly she could never carry it. She would take in the tea-things one by one, even if it took half-an-hour.

She did this, resting only once between her journeys. First the tea-pot, which she placed on the library hearth. Then the hot-water jug. These were the dangerous objects. Cup and saucer; another cup and saucer in case Godfrey or Mrs. Pettigrew should return and want tea; the buttered scones; jam; two plates, two knives, and two spoons. Another journey for the plate of Garibaldi biscuits which Charmian loved to dip in her tea. She could well remember, as she looked at them, the fuss about Garibaldi in her childhood, and her father's eloquent letters to *The Times* which were read aloud after morning prayers. Three of the Garibaldi biscuits slid off the plate and broke on the floor in the hall. She proceeded with the plate, laid it on a table, and then returned to pick up the broken biscuits, even the crumbs. It would be a pity if anyone said she had been careless. Still, she felt fearless that afternoon. Last of all she went to fetch the tray itself, with its pretty cloth. She stopped to mop up the water she had spilt by the stove. When she had brought everything into the room she closed the door, placed the tray on a low table by her chair and arranged her tea-things neatly upon it. The performance had taken twenty minutes. She dozed with gratitude in her chair for five more minutes, then carefully poured out her tea, splashing very little into the saucer. Even that little she eventually poured back into the cup. All was as usual, save that she was blissfully alone, and the tea was not altogether hot. She started to enjoy her tea.

Mrs. Pettigrew stood under the chipped stucco of the porch and looked at her watch. She could not see the dial in the gloom. She walked down the steps and consulted her watch under a lamp-post. It was twenty to five. She turned to resume her station in the bombed porch. She had mounted two steps when, from nowhere, a policeman appeared.

"Anything you wanted, madam?"

"Oh, I'm waiting for a friend."

He went up the steps and pushing open the creaking door flashed his torch all over the interior, as if expecting her friend to be there. He gave her a curious look and walked away.

Mrs. Pettigrew thought, It's too bad, it really is, me being put in a predicament like this, standing in the cold, questioned by policemen; and I'm nearly seventy-four. Something rustled on the ground behind the door. She looked; she could see nothing. But then she felt something, like the stroke of a hand over her instep. She shuffled backwards, and catching the last glimpse of a rat slithering through the railings down the area, screamed.

The policeman crossed over the street towards her, having apparently been watching her from some doorway on the other side.

"Anything wrong?" he said.

"A rat," she said, "ran across my feet."

"I shouldn't stand here, madam, please."

"I'm waiting for my friend. Go away."

"What's your name, madam?"

She thought he said, "What's your game?" and it occurred to her, too, that she probably looked years younger than she thought. "You can have three guesses," she replied pertly.

"I must ask you to move along, madam. Where do you live?"

"Suppose you mind your own business?"

"Got anyone to look after you?" he said; and she realised he had not much underestimated her years, but probably suspected she was dotty.

"I'm waiting for my friend," she said.

The policeman stood uncertainly before her, considering her face, and possibly what to do about her. There was a slight stir behind the door. Mrs. Pettigrew jumped nervously. "Oh, is that a rat?"

Just then a car door slammed behind the policeman's bulk.

"That's my friend," she said, trying to slip past him. "Let me pass, please."

The policeman turned to scrutinise the car. Godfrey was already driving off.

"Godfrey! Godfrey!" she called. But he was away.

"Your friend didn't stop long," he observed.

"I've missed him through you talking to me."

She started off down the steps.

"Think you'll get home all right?" The policeman seemed relieved to see her moving off.

She did not reply but got a taxi at King's Road, thinking how hard used she was.

Godfrey, on her arrival, was expostulating with Charmian. "I say you *couldn't* have made the tea and brought it in here. How could you? Mrs. Pettigrew brought in your tea. Now think. You've been dreaming."

Charmian turned to Mrs. Pettigrew. "You have been out all afternoon, haven't you, Mrs. Pettigrew?"

"Mabel," said Mrs. Pettigrew.

"Haven't you, Mabel? I made my tea myself and brought it in. Godfrey won't believe me, he's absurd."

"I brought in your tea," said Mrs. Pettigrew, "before I went out for an airing. I must say I feel the need of it these days since Mrs. Anthony started leaving early."

"You see what I mean?" said Godfrey to Charmian.

Charmian was silent.

"A whole long story," said Godfrey, "about getting up and making your own tea. I knew it was impossible."

Charmian said, "I am getting feeble in mind as well

as body, Godfrey. I shall go to the nursing home in Surrey. I am quite decided."

"Perhaps," said Mrs. Pettigrew, "that would be the best."

"There's no need, my dear, for you to go into a home," said Godfrey. "No one is suggesting it. All I was saying—"

"I'm going to bed, Godfrey."

"Oh, dear, a supper tray," said Mrs. Pettigrew.

"I don't want supper, thank you," said Charmian. "I enjoyed my tea."

Mrs. Pettigrew moved towards Charmian as if to take her arm.

"I can manage quite well, thank you."

"Come now, don't get into a tantrum. You must get your beauty sleep for the photographer to-morrow," said Mrs. Pettigrew.

Charmian made her slow way out of the room and upstairs.

"See the lawyer?" said Mrs. Pettigrew.

"It's damn cold," said Godfrey.

"You saw the solicitor?"

"No, in fact, he'd been called away on an urgent case. Have to see him some other time. I say I'll see him to-morrow, Mabel."

"Urgent case," she said. "It was the lawyer you had an appointment with, not the doctor. You're worse than Charmian."

"Yes, yes, Mabel, the lawyer. Don't let Mrs. Anthony hear you."

"Mrs. Anthony has gone. And, anyway, she's deaf. Where have you been all afternoon?"

"Well, I called in," he said, "at the police."

"What?"

"The police station. Kept me waiting a long time."

"Look here, Godfrey, you have no evidence against me,

you understand? You need proof. Just you try. What did you tell them? Come on, what did you say?"

"Can't remember exact words. Time they did something about it. I said, 'My sister has been suffering from this man for over six months.' I said, 'Now he has started on me,' I said, 'and it's high time you did something about it,' I said. I said—"

"Oh, your phone call. Is that all you have to think about? I ask you, Godfrey, is *that all* . . . ?"

He huddled in his chair. "Damn cold," he said. "Have we got any whisky there?"

"No," she said, "we haven't."

He silently opened Charmian's door on his way to bed. "Still awake?" he said in a whisper.

"Yes," she said, waking up.

"Feeling all right? Want anything?"

"Nothing, thank you, Godfrey."

"Don't go to the nursing home," he said in a whisper.

"Godfrey, I made my own tea this afternoon."

"All right," he said, "you did. But don't go—"

"Godfrey," she said. "If you will take my advice you will write to Eric. You will make it up with Eric."

"Why? What makes you say that?"

But she would not say what made her say this, and he was puzzled by it, for he himself had been thinking of writing to Eric; he was uncertain whether Charmian knew more about him and his plight than he thought, or whether her words represented merely a stray idea.

"You must promise," said Olive Mannering, "that this is to be treated as a strictly professional matter."

"I promise," said Alec Warner.

"Because," said Olive, "it's dangerous stuff, and I got it in strictest confidence. And I wouldn't tell a soul."

"Nor I," said Alec.

"It's only for purposes of research," said Olive.

"Quite."

"How do you make your notes?" Olive enquired. "Because there mustn't be names mentioned anywhere."

"All documents referring to real names are to be destroyed at my death. No one could possibly identify my case-histories."

"O.K.," said Olive. "Well, goodness, he was in a terrible state this afternoon. I was really sorry for him. It's Mrs. Pettigrew, you see."

"Garters and all that lark?"

"No, oh no. He's finished with that."

"Blackmail."

"That's right. She has apparently discovered a lot about his past life."

"The affair with Lisa Brooke."

"That and a lot more. Then there was some money scandal at the Colston Breweries which was hushed up at the time. Mrs. Pettigrew knows it all. She got at his private papers."

"Has he been to the police?"

"No, he's afraid."

"They would protect him. What is he afraid of? Did you ask?"

"His wife, mostly. He doesn't want his wife to know. It's his pride, I think. Of course, I haven't met her but it sounds to me that she's always been the religious one, and being famous as an author off and on, she gets all the sympathy for being more sensitive than him."

Alec Warner wrote in his book.

"Charmian," he remarked, "would not be put out by anything she learnt about Godfrey. Now, you say he's *afraid* of her knowing?"

"Yes, he is, really."

"Most people," he said, "would say she was afraid of him. He bullies her."

"Well, I've only heard his side. He looks pretty bad just now."

"Did you notice the complexion?"

"High coloured. Goodness he's lost weight."

"Stooping more?"

"Oh, much more. The stuffing's knocked out of him. Mrs. Pettigrew keeps the whisky locked up."

Alec made a note. "Do him good in the long run," he commented. "He drank too much for his age. What is he going to do about Mrs. Pettigrew?"

"Well, he pays up. But she keeps demanding more. He hates paying up. And the latest thing, she wants him to make a new will in her favour. He was supposed to be at the lawyer to-day, but he called in on me instead. He thought I might persuade Eric to come and frighten her. He says Eric wouldn't lose by it. But as you know, Eric feels very bitter about his family, and he's jealous of his mother, especially since her novels are in print again, and the fact is, Eric is entitled to a certain amount, it's only a question of time. . . ."

"Eric," said Alec, "is not one of us. Go on about Godfrey."

"He says he'd like to make it up with Eric. I promised to write to Eric for him, and so I shall, but as I say—"

"Has Mrs. Pettigrew any money of her own?"

"Oh, I don't know. You never know with a woman like that, do you? I don't think she has much, because of something I heard yesterday."

"What was that?"

"Well," said Olive, "I got the story from Ronald Sidebottome, he called yesterday. I didn't get it from Godfrey."

"What was the story?" said Alec. "You know, Olive, I always pay extra if it entails an extra interview on your part."

"O.K.," said Olive, "keep your hair on. I just wanted you to know this makes another item."

Alec smiled at her like an uncle.

"Ronald Sidebottome," she said, "has finally decided not to contest Lisa Brooke's will now that Tempest is dead. The case was really Tempest's idea. He said the whole thing would have been very distasteful. All about Lisa's marriage with Guy Leet not being consummated. Mrs. Pettigrew is awfully angry about the case being withdrawn, because she was working in with the Sidebottomes when Tempest died. And she hasn't managed to get her hold on Ronald, though she's been trying hard all winter. Ronald is a very independent type at heart. You don't know old Ronald. He's deaf, I admit, but—"

"I have known Ronald over forty years. How interesting he should strike you as an independent type."

"He has a nice way with him on the quiet," she said. She had met Ronald Sidebottome while strolling round a picture gallery with her grandfather shortly after Tempest's death, and had brought the two old men back to supper. "But if you've known Ronald for forty years, then you don't want to hear any more from me."

"My dear, I have known Ronald over forty years but I can't know him as you do."

"He hates Mrs. Pettigrew," Olive observed with an inward-musing smile. "She won't get much of Lisa's bequest. All she has so far is Lisa's squirrel coat, that's all."

"Does she think of contesting the will on her own account?"

"No, she's been advised her case is too weak. Mrs. Brooke paid her adequately all the time; there's no case. Anyway, I don't think she has the capital to finance it. She was depending on the Sidebottomes. Of course, under the will, the money goes to her when Guy Leet dies. But he's telling everyone how fit he feels. So you can be sure

Mrs. P. is going to get all she can out of poor old Godfrey."

Alec Warner finished his notes and closed the book. Olive passed him a drink.

"Poor old Godfrey," said Olive. "And he was upset by something else, too. He had an anonymous phone call from that man who worries his sister—or at least he thinks he had. It amounts to the same thing, doesn't it?"

Alec Warner opened his notebook again and got his pen from the pocket of his waistcoat. "What did the man say?"

"The same thing. 'You are going to die' or something."

"Always be exact. Dame Lettie's man says, 'Remember you must die'—Was that what Godfrey heard?"

"I think so," she said. "This sort of work is very tiring."

"I know, my dear. It must be. What time of day did he receive this call?"

"The morning. That I do know. He told me it was just after the doctor had left Charmian."

Alec completed his notes and closed his book once more. He said to Olive, "Has Guy Leet been informed of the withdrawal of the law-suit?"

"I don't know. The decision was only made yesterday afternoon."

"Perhaps he does not know yet," said Alec. "Lisa's money will make a great difference to a man of Guy's tastes. He has been feeling the pinch lately."

"He can't have long to live," said Olive.

"Lisa's money will make his short time pleasanter. I take it this information is not particularly confidential?"

"No," said Olive, "only what I told you of Mrs. Pettigrew's hold on Godfrey—that's confidential."

Alec Warner went home and wrote a letter to Guy Leet:

Dear Guy—I do not know if I am the first to inform you that neither Ronald Sidebottome nor Mrs. Pettigrew are now proceeding with their suit in contest of Lisa's will.

I offer you my congratulations, and trust you will long enjoy your good fortune.

Forgive me for thus attempting to anticipate an official notification. If I have been successful in being the first to convey this news to you, will you kindly oblige me by taking your pulse and your temperature immediately upon reading this letter, and again one hour afterwards, and again the following morning, and inform me of the same, together with your normal pulse-rate and temperature if you know it?

This will be invaluable for my records. I shall be so much obliged.

Yours,
Alec Warner

P.S. Any additional observations as to your reaction to the good news will of course be much appreciated.

Alec Warner went to post the letter and returned to write up his records. Twice, the telephone rang. The first call was from Godfrey Colston, whose record-card, as it happened, Alec held in his hand.

"Oh," said Godfrey, "you're in."

"Yes. Have you been trying to get me?"

"No," said Godfrey. "Look here, I want to speak to you. Do you know anyone in the police?"

"Not well," said Alec, "since Mortimer retired."

"Mortimer's no good," said Godfrey. "It's about these anonymous calls. Mortimer has been looking into them for months. Now the chap has started on me."

"I have an hour to spare between nine and ten. Can you come round to the club?"

Alec returned to his notes. The second telephone call came a quarter of an hour later. It was from a man who said, "Remember you must die."

"Would you mind repeating that?" said Alec.

The speaker repeated it.

"Thank you," said Alec, and replaced the receiver a fraction before the other had done so.

He got out his own card and made an entry. Then he made a cross-reference to another card which he duly annotated. Finally he wrote a passage in his diary, ending it with the words, "Query: mass-hysteria."

Chapter Eleven

In the fine new sunshine of April which fell upon her through the window, Emmeline Mortimer adjusted her glasses and smoothed her blouse. She was grateful to be free of her winter jumpers and to wear a blouse and cardigan again.

She decided to sow parsley that morning and perhaps set out the young carnations and the sweet peas. Perhaps Henry would prune the roses. Henry was over the worst, but she must not let him hoe or weed or in any way strain or stoop. She must keep an eye on him without appearing to do so. This evening, when the people had gone he could spray the gooseberries with lime-sulphur in case of mildew and the pears with Bordeaux mixture in case of scab. And the black-currants in case of big bud again. There was so much to be done, and Henry must not overdo it. No, he must not spray the pears for he might over-reach and strain himself. The people would certainly exhaust him.

Her hearing was sharp that morning. Henry was moving about briskly upstairs. He was humming. The scent of her hyacinths on the window ledge came in brief irregular waves which she received with a sharp and pleasant pang. She sipped her warm and splendid tea and adjusted the cosy round the pot, keeping it hot for Henry. She touched her glasses into focus and turned to the morning paper.

Henry Mortimer came down in a few moments. His wife turned her head very slightly when he came in and returned to her paper.

He opened the french windows and stood there for a while satisfying his body with the new sun and air and his eyes with his garden. Then he closed the windows and took his place at the table. "A bit of hoeing to-day," he said.

She made no immediate objection, for she must bide her time. Not that Henry was touchy or difficult about his angina. It was more a matter of principle and habit; she had always waited her time before opposing any statement of Henry's.

He gestured with the back of his hand towards the sunny weather. "What d'you think of it?" he said.

She looked up, smiled, and nodded once. Her face was a network of fine wrinkles except where the skin was stretched across her small sharp bones. Her back was straight, her figure neat, and her movements easy. One half of her mind was busy calculating the number of places she would have to set for the people this afternoon. She was four years older than Henry, who had turned seventy at the beginning of February. His first heart attack had followed soon after, and Henry, half-inclined to envisage his doctor as a personification of his illness, had declared himself much improved since the doctor had ceased to pay regular daily visits. He had been allowed up for afternoons, then for whole days. The doctor had bade him not to worry, always to carry his box of tablets, to stick to his diet, and to avoid any exertion. The doctor had told Emmeline to ring him any time if necessary. And then, to Henry's relief, the doctor had disappeared from the house.

Henry Mortimer, the former Chief Inspector, was long, lean, bald and spritely. At the sides and back of his head his hair grew thick and grey. His eyebrows were thick and black. It would be accurate to say that his nose and lips were thick, his eyes small and his chin receding into his neck. And yet it would be inaccurate to say he was not a handsome man, such being the power of unity when it exists in a face.

He scraped butter sparingly on his toast in deference to the departed doctor, and remarked to his wife, "I've got these people coming this afternoon."

She said, "There's another bit about them in the paper to-day." And she held her peace for the meantime about his having to take care not to wear himself out with them; for what was the point of his being retired from the Force if he continued to lay himself out on criminal cases?

He stretched out his hand and she put the paper into it. "Hoax Caller Strikes Again," he read aloud. Then he read on to himself:

Police are still mystified by continued complaints of a number of elderly people who have been receiving anonymous telephone calls from a male hoax-caller since August last year.

There may be more than one man behind the hoax. Reports on the type of voice vary from "very young," "middle-aged" to "elderly" etc.

The voice invariably warns the victim, "You will die to-night."

The aged victims' telephones are being tapped by the authorities, and police have requested them to keep the caller in conversation if possible. But this, and all other methods of detecting hoax-callers have so far failed, the police admitted yesterday.

It was thought at first that the gang's activities were confined to the Central London area. But a recent report from former critic Mr. Guy Leet, 75, of Stedrost, Surrey, indicates that the net is spreading wider.

Among numerous others previously reported to be recipients of "the Call" are Dame Lettie Colston, O.B.E., 79, pioneer penal reformer, and her sister-in-law Charmian Piper (Mrs. Godfrey Colston) the novelist, 85, author of *The Seventh Child*, etc.

Dame Lettie told reporters yesterday, "I am not satisfied that the C.I.D. have taken these incidents seriously enough. I am employing a private agency. I consider it a great pity that flogging has been abolished. These vile creatures ought to be taught a lesson."

Charmian Piper, whose husband, Mr. Godfrey Colston, 86, former Chairman of Colston Breweries, is also among the victims of the hoax, said yesterday, "We are not in the least perturbed by the caller. He is a very civil young man."

A C.I.D. spokesman said everything possible is being done to discover the offender.

Henry Mortimer put down the paper and took the cup his wife was passing him.

"An extraordinary sort of case," she said.

"Embarrassing for the police," he said, "poor fellows."

"Oh, they'll get the culprit, won't they?"

"I don't see," he said, "how they ever can, all evidence considered."

"Well, you know the evidence, of course."

"And considering the evidence," he said, "in my opinion the offender is Death himself."

She was not really surprised to hear him say this. She had followed his mind all through its conforming life and late independence, so that nothing he said could surprise her very much. He had lived to see his children cease to take him seriously—his word carried more force in the outside world. Even his older grand-children, though they loved him, would never now understand his value to others. He knew this; he did not care. Emmeline could never, however, regard Henry as a dear old thing who had taken to developing a philosophy, as other men, on their retirement, might cultivate a hobby. She did not entirely let her children see how she felt, for she liked to please them and seem solid and practical in their eyes. But she trusted Henry, and she could not help doing so.

She let him busy himself in the garden before she sent him indoors to rest. A few more weeks and he would be watching the post for that particular letter from his old friend in the country inviting him to come for a fortnight's fishing. It seemed miraculous that another spring had begun and that soon Henry would announce, "I've heard from Harry. The *mayfly's* on the river. I'd better be off day after tomorrow." Then she would be alone for a while, or perhaps one of the girls would come to stay after Easter and the younger children would roll over and over on the lawn if it was dry enough.

She sowed her parsley, and wondered excitedly what the deputation who were calling to see Henry this afternoon would look like.

The Mortimers' house at Kingston-on-Thames was not difficult to reach, if one followed Henry's directions. However the deputation had found it a difficult place to find. They arrived shaken in nerve and body, half an hour late in Godfrey's car and two taxis. In Godfrey's car, besides Godfrey himself, were Charmian, Dame Lettie and Mrs. Pettigrew. The first taxi bore Alec Warner and Dame Lettie's maid, Gwen. In the second taxi came Janet Sidebottome, that missionary sister of Lisa Brooke; accompanying her were an elderly couple and an aged spinster who were strangers to the rest.

Mrs. Pettigrew, spruce and tailor-made, stepped out first. Henry Mortimer came beaming down the path and shook her hand. Godfrey emerged next, and meantime there was a general exit from the two taxis, and a fussy finding and counting of money for the fares.

Charmian, from the back of Godfrey's car, said, "Oh, I have so enjoyed the drive. My first this year. The river is splendid to-day."

"Wait a minute, wait a minute, Godfrey," said Dame Lettie who was being helped out. "Don't pull me." She had grown stouter and yet more fragile during the past winter. Her sight was failing, and it was obviously difficult for her to find the kerb with her foot. "Wait, Godfrey."

"We're late," said Godfrey. "Charmian, sit still, don't move till we've got Lettie out."

Mrs. Pettigrew took Dame Lettie's other arm while Henry Mortimer stood holding the door. Lettie yanked her arm away from Mrs. Pettigrew, so that her handbag dropped to the pavement and the contents spilled out. The occupants of the taxis rushed to rescue Lettie's belongings, while Lettie herself drew back into the car and sank with a plump sound into her seat.

Young Gwen, whom Dame Lettie had brought as a witness, stood in the gateway and laughed aloud.

Mrs. Mortimer came briskly down the path and addressed Gwen. "Look lively, young person," she said, "and help your elders instead of standing there laughing."

Gwen looked surprised and did not move.

"Go and pick up your aunt's belongings," said Mrs. Mortimer.

Dame Lettie, fearful of losing her maid, called out from the car,

"I'm not her aunt, Mrs. Mortimer. It's all right, Gwen."

Mrs. Mortimer, who was not normally an irate woman, took Gwen by the shoulders and propelled her over to the little group who were stiffly bending to retrieve the contents of the bag. "Let the girl pick them up," she said.

Most of the things were, however by now collected, and while Alec Warner, directed by Henry Mortimer, stooped to fish with his umbrella under the car for Dame Lettie's spectacle-case, Gwen so far overcame her surprise as to say to Mrs. Mortimer, "I got nothing to do with *you*."

"All right, Gwen. It's all right," said Dame Lettie from the car.

Mrs. Mortimer now kept her peace although it was clear she would have liked to say more to Gwen. She had been troubled, in the first place, by the sight of these infirm and agitated people arriving with such difficulty at her door. Where are their children? she had thought, or their nieces and nephews? Why are they left to their own resources like this?

She edged Gwen aside and reached into the car for Dame Lettie's arm. At the opposite door Henry Mortimer was reaching for Charmian's. Mrs. Mortimer, as she assisted Dame Lettie, hoped he would not strain himself, and said to Dame Lettie, "I see you have brought the spring weather." As Lettie finally came to rest on the pavement Mrs. Mortimer looked up to see Alec Warner's eyes upon her. She thought, That man is studying me for some reason.

Charmian tottered gaily up the path on Henry Mortimer's arm. He was telling her he had just read, once more, her novel *The Gates of Grandella* in its fine new edition.

"It is over fifty years," said Charmian, "since *I* read it."

"It captures the period," said Mortimer. "Oh, it brings everything back. I do recommend you to read it again."

Charmian slid her eyes flirtatiously towards him—that gesture which the young reporters who came to see her found so enchanting—and said, "You are too young, Henry, to remember when the book first came out."

"No indeed," he said, "I was already a police constable. And a constable never forgets."

"What a charming house," said Charmian, and she

caught sight of Godfrey waiting inside the hall, and felt she was, as always when people made a fuss over her, making him sick.

The conference did not start for some time. Emmeline Mortimer consulted in low tones with the ladies of the deputation in the hall, whether they would first like to go "upstairs," or, if the stairs were too much for them, there was a place downstairs, straight through the kitchen, turn right. "Charmian," said Mrs. Pettigrew out loud, "come and make yourself comfortable. I'll take you. Come along."

Henry Mortimer piled the men's coats and hats neatly on a chest, and, having shown the way upstairs to the male candidates, ushered the rest of the men into the dining-room where, at the long table, bare except for a vase of shining daffodils, and at the top, a thick file of papers, Gwen was already seated, fuming sulkily to herself.

When Godfrey came in he glanced round at the furnishings with an enquiring air.

"Is this the right room?" he said.

Alec Warner thought: He is probably looking for signs of a tea-tray. He probably thinks we are not going to get any tea.

"Yes, I think this is most suitable," said Henry, as one taking him into consultation. "Don't you? We can sit round the table and talk things over before tea."

"Oh!" said Godfrey. Alec Warner congratulated himself.

At last they were settled round the table, the three strangers having been introduced as a Miss Lottinville and a Mr. and Mrs. Jack Rose. Mrs. Mortimer withdrew and the door clicked behind her like a signal for the start of business. The sunlight fell mildly upon the table and the people round it, showing up motes of dust in the air, specks of dust on the clothes of those who wore black, the wrinkled cheeks and hands of the aged, and the thick make-up of Gwen.

Charmian, who was enthroned in the most comfortable chair, spoke first, "What a charming room."

"It gets the afternoon sun," Henry said. "Is it too much for anyone? Charmian—another cushion."

The three strangers looked uneasily at each other, simply because they were strangers and not, like the others, known to each other for forty, fifty years it might be.

Godfrey moved his arm to shoot back his sleeve, and said, "This telephone man, Mortimer, I must say, it's a bit thick—"

"I have a copy of your statement here, Colston," said Henry Mortimer, opening his file. "I propose to read each one aloud by turn, and you may add any further comments after I have read it. Does that course meet with approval?"

No one seriously disagreed with that course.

Gwen looked out of the window. Janet Sidebottome fiddled with the electric battery of her elaborate hearing-aid. Mrs. Pettigrew laid her arm on the table and her chin on her hand and looked intense. Charmian sat with her heart-shaped face composed beneath her new blue hat. Alec Warner looked carefully at the strangers, first at Mrs. Rose then at Mr. Rose and then at Miss Lottinville. Mrs. Rose had her eyebrows perpetually raised in resignation, furrowing deep lines into her forehead. Mr. Rose held his head sideways; he had enormous shoulders; his large mouth drooped downwards at the same degree of curvature as his chin, cheeks and nose. The Roses must be nearly eighty, perhaps more. Miss Lottinville looked small and slight and angry. The left side of her mouth and her right eye kept twitching simultaneously.

Henry Mortimer's voice was not too official, but it was firm:

". . . just after eleven in the morning . . . on three separate occasions . . . It sounded like that of a common man. The tone was menacing. The words on each occasion were . . ."

". . . at various times throughout the day . . . the first occasion was on 12th March. The words were . . . The tone was strictly factual. . . . He sounded young, like a Teddy-boy. . . ."

". . . first thing in the morning . . . every week since the end of August last. It was the voice of a cultured, middle-aged man . . . the tone is sinister in the extreme. . . ."

"It was the voice of a very civil young man. . . ." This was Charmian's account. Godfrey broke in. "How could he be a civil young man saying a thing like that? Use your head, Charmian."

"He was," said Charmian, "most civil on all three occasions."

"Perhaps," said Henry, "if I could continue . . . ? Then Charmian can add her comments."

He finished Charmian's statement. "That is correct," said Charmian.

"How could he be *civil?*" said Godfrey.

"Mr. Guy Leet," Henry announced, taking up the next paper. "Oh, Guy isn't here, of course—"

"Guy asked me to say," said Alec, "we could discuss his case as much as we like so long as we don't discuss his private life up to 1940."

"Has to get about on two sticks," commented Godfrey.

"Guy's account," said Henry, "is substantially the same as the others, with the most interesting exception that he gets Tol calls from London at between six and seven in the evening when the cheap rate is on. In his opinion the offender is a schoolboy."

"Nonsense," said Dame Lettie. "A middle-aged man."

"It is simple," said Henry, "to trace a Tol call from London to the country. And yet the police have not yet traced any caller to Guy Leet at Stedrost."

"Quite," said Dame Lettie. "The police—"

"However, we will discuss these factors later," said Henry. "Next Mr. Ronald Sidebottome— Oh, Ronald's not here either. What's happened to Ronald, Janet?"

"He was a youth—a Teddy-boy, as I've said," Janet Sidebottome replied.

"Ronald" roared Godfrey into her ear. "Why hasn't Ronald turned up? He said he was coming."

"Oh, Ronald. Well, he was to call for me. I suppose he forgot. It was most annoying. I waited and then I rang him up but he wasn't at home. I really can't answer for Ronald these days. He is never at home."

Alec Warner took out a small diary and scribbled something in pencil.

"Ronald's statement," said Mortimer, "describes the caller as a man well advanced in years with a cracked and rather shaky voice and a suppliant tone."

"There must be something wrong with his phone," said Dame Lettie. "The man's voice is strong and sinister. A man of middle years. You must remember, Henry, that I have had far more experience of the creature than anyone else."

"Yes, Lettie, my dear, I admit you have been greatly tried. Now Miss Lottinville, your statement . . . 'At three o'clock in the morning . . . A foreigner . . .' "

Mrs. Mortimer put her head round the door. "Tea is ready, Henry, when you are. I have laid it in the breakfast room so that—'

"In five minutes, Emmeline."

She disappeared and Godfrey looked yearningly after her.

"Finally, Mr. Rose," said Henry. " 'I received the call at my business premises at twelve noon on two days running . . . the man sounded like an official person . . . late middle age. . . .' "

"That sounds accurate," said Dame Lettie. "Only I would describe the voice as *sinister*."

"Did he have a lisp?" said Godfrey.

"Mr. Rose has not mentioned a lisp in his statement— Had he a lisp, Mr. Rose?" said Henry.

"No, no. Like an official. My wife says an army man, but I would say a government chap."

Everyone spoke at once.

"Oh no," said Janet Sidebottome, "he was—"

"A gang," said Dame Lettie, "there must be a gang."

Miss Lottinville said: "I assure you, Chief Inspector, he—"

Henry waited for a while till the noise subsided. He said to Mr. Rose,

"Are you satisfied with your account as I have read it?"

"A hundred per cent," said Mr. Rose.

"Then let's continue the discussion after tea," said Henry.

Miss Lottinville said: "You have not read the statement of this lady on my left." The lady on her left was Mrs. Pettigrew. "*I* haven't had any of your phone calls," she said. "I've made no statement."

Alec Warner wondered, from the vehemence of her tone, if she were lying.

Mrs. Mortimer sat with her silver tea-pot poised at a well-spread table.

"Come and sit by me," she said kindly to Gwen, "and you can help to pass the cups."

Gwen lit a cigarette and sat down sideways at the place indicated.

"Have you been afflicted with these phone calls?" Emmeline Mortimer asked her.

"Me? No, I get wrong numbers."

Mrs. Pettigrew said confidentially to Mrs. Mortimer: "I've had no trouble myself from any phone calls. Between ourselves, I think it's all made up. I don't believe a word of what they say. They're trying to draw attention to themselves. Like kids."

"What a delightful garden," said Charmian.

They were assembled once more in the dining-room where a fire sparkled weakly in the sunlight.

Henry Mortimer said: "If I had my life over again I should form the habit of nightly composing myself to thoughts of death. I would practise, as it were, the remembrance of death. There is no other practise which so intensifies life. Death, when it approaches, ought not to take one by surprise. It should be part of the full expectancy of life. Without an ever-present sense of death life is insipid. You might as well live on the whites of eggs."

Dame Lettie said suddenly and sharply, "Who is the man, Henry?"

"My dear Lettie. I can't help you, there."

She looked so closely at him, he felt almost that she suspected himself.

"Lettie thinks you are the man," said Alec wickedly.

"I hardly think," said Henry, "Lettie would attribute to me such energy and application as the culprit evidently possesses."

"All we want," said Godfrey, "is to stop him. And to do that we've got to find the man."

"I consider," said Janet Sidebottome, "that what Mr. Mortimer was saying just now about resigning ourselves to death is most uplifting and consoling. The religious point of view is too easily forgotten these days, and I thank you, Mr. Mortimer."

"Why, thank you, Janet. Perhaps 'resigning ourselves to death' doesn't quite convey what I mean. But of course, I don't attempt to express a specifically religious point of view. My observations were merely confined—"

"You sound most religious to me," said Janet.

"Thank you, Janet."

"Poor young man," mused Charmian. "He may be lonely, and simply wanting to talk to people and so he rings them up."

"The police, of course, are hopeless. Really, Henry, it is time there was a question in the House," said Lettie warningly.

"Considering the fairly wide discrepancies in your various reports," said Henry, "the police at one stage in their investigations assumed that not one man but a gang was at work. The police have, however, employed every method of detection known to criminology and science, so far without success. Now, one factor is constant in all your reports. The words, 'Remember you must die.' It is, you know, an excellent thing to remember this, for it is nothing more than the truth. To remember one's death is, in short, a way of life."

"To come to the point—" said Godfrey.

"Godfrey," said Charmian, "I am sure everyone is fascinated by what Henry is saying."

"Most consoling," said Janet Sidebottome. "Do continue, Mr. Mortimer, with your words."

"Ah yes," said Miss Lottinville who was also enjoying Henry's philosophising.

And Mrs. Rose, with her longanimous eyes and resignation, nodded her head in sad, wise and ancient assent.

"Have you considered," said Alec Warner, "the possibility of mass hysteria?"

"Making telephones ring?" said Mr. Rose, spreading wide his palms.

"Absurd!" said Dame Lettie. "We can eliminate mass hysteria."

"Oh no," said Mortimer. "In a case like this we can't eliminate any possibility. That is just our difficulty."

"Tell me," Alec asked the Chief Inspector with his piercing look, "would you describe yourself as a mystic?"

"Never having previously been called upon to describe myself, I really couldn't say."

"The question is," said Mr. Rose, "who's the fellow that's trying to put the fear of God in us?"

"And what's the motive?" said Godfrey. "That's what I ask."

"The question of motive may prove to be different in each case, to judge by the evidence before us," said Mortimer. "I think we must all realise that the offender is, in each case, whoever we think he is ourselves."

"Did you tell them," said Emmeline Mortimer when they had gone, "what your theory is?"

"No—oh no, my dear. I treated them to brief philosophical sermons instead. It helped to pass the time."

"Did they like your little sermons?"

"Some of the women did. The young girl seemed less bored than at other times. Lettie objected."

"Oh, Lettie."

"She said the whole afternoon had been pointless."

"How rude. After my lovely tea."

"It was a lovely tea. It was my part that was pointless. I'm afraid it had to be."

"How I wish," said Emmeline, "you could have told them outright, 'Death is the culprit.' And I should like to have seen their faces."

"It's a personal opinion. One can't make up one's mind for others."

"Can they make up their own minds, then?"

"No. I think I'll go and spray the pears."

"Now, darling," said Mrs. Mortimer. "You know you've done enough for one day. I'm sure it's been quite enough for me."

"The trouble with these people," he said, "they think that the C.I.D. are God, understanding all mysteries and all knowledge. Whereas we are only policemen."

He went to read by the fire in the dining-room. Before he sat down he straightened the chairs round the table and put back some of them in their places round the wall. He emptied the ash-trays into the fire. He looked out of the window at the half-light and hoped for a fine summer. He had not mentioned it to Emmeline yet, but this summer he hoped to sail that yacht of his for which, in his retirement, he had sacrificed a car. Already he could feel the bright wet wind about his ears.

The telephone rang. He went out to the hall, answered it. Within a few seconds he put down the receiver. How strange, he thought, that mine is always a woman. Everyone else gets a man on the line to them, but mine is always this woman, gentle-spoken and respectful.

Chapter Twelve

"I told him straight what I feel," said Mrs. Pettigrew to Mrs. Anthony. "I said, 'It's all a lot of rot, Inspector. It started with Dame Lettie Colston, then Godfrey feels he's got to be in the picture and one sets off the other. To my dying day I'll swear it's all make up.' But he didn't side with me. Why? I'll tell you why. He'd be put out of Dame Lettie's will if he agreed it was all her imagination."

Mrs. Pettigrew, though she had in fact, once quiet afternoon, received the anonymous telephone call, had chosen to forget it. She possessed a strong faculty for simply refusing to admit an unpleasant situation, and to go quite blank where it was concerned. If, for instance, you had asked her whether, eighteen years before she had undergone a face-lifting operation, she would have denied it, and believed the denial, and moreover would have supplied gratuitously, as a special joke, a list of people who had, "really" had their faces lifted or undergone other rejuvenating operations.

And so Mrs. Pettigrew continued to persuade herself she had not heard the anonymous voice on the telephone; it was not a plain ignoring of the incident; she omitted even to keep a mental record of it, but put down the receiver and blacked it out from her life.

"A lot of imagination all round," said Mrs. Pettigrew.

"Ah well," said Mrs. Anthony, "we all got to go some

day. But I shouldn't like to have that chap on the phone to me. I'd give him something to get along with."

"There isn't any chap," said Mrs. Pettigrew. "You hear what I say?"

"I got my deaf-aid in, and I hear what you say. No need to raise your voice."

Mrs. Pettigrew was overcome by that guilt she felt whenever she had lowered herself to the intimacy of shouting at Mrs. Anthony, forgetting to play her cards. By way of recompense she left the kitchen aloofly, and went to find Godfrey.

He was sitting by the fire, maddeningly, opposite Charmian.

"Please, Godfrey, let us not have all this over again. Ah, it's you, Mrs. Pettigrew," said Charmian.

"She is not Taylor," said Godfrey, with automatic irritability.

"I know it," said Charmian.

He looked unhappily at Mrs. Pettigrew. There was really no consolation left in the house for a man. He was all the more disturbed by Charmian's increasing composure. It was not that he wished his wife any harm, but his spirits always seemed to wither in proportion as hers bloomed. He thought, looking at his wife, It is only for a time, this can't last, she will have a relapse. He felt he was an old man in difficulties. Mrs. Pettigrew had made another appointment for his lawyer that afternoon. He did not feel up to keeping it. He supposed he would have to see the lawyer some time, but that long fruitless going to and from Kingston yesterday had left him exhausted. And that madman Mortimer, making a fuss over Charmian—everyone making a fuss over Charmian, as if she were still somebody and not a helpless old invalid—roused within him all those resentments of the long past; so that, having made the mistake of regarding Charmian's every success as his failure, now, by force of habit, he could never feel really well unless she were ill.

Charmian was saying to him, "We did talk over the whole matter quite a lot last night. Let us leave the subject alone. I for one like Henry Mortimer, and I thoroughly enjoyed the drive."

Mrs. Pettigrew, too, was alarmed by this mental recovery of Charmian's, induced apparently, by the revival of those old books. In reality it was also, in part, due to an effortful will to resist Mrs. Pettigrew's bullying. Mrs. Pettigrew felt that there might now even be some chance of Charmian's outliving Godfrey. Charmian should be in a home, and would be, if Godfrey were not weak-minded about it, trying to play on his wife's sympathy and keep her with him.

Godfrey looked across the fireplace at his ally and enemy, Charmian, and at Mabel Pettigrew, whom he so tremendously feared, sitting between them, and decided to give Mrs. Pettigrew the slip again this afternoon and go to see Olive.

Mabel Pettigrew thought: I can read him like a book. She had not read a book for over forty years, could never concentrate on reading, but this nevertheless was her thought; and she decided to accompany him to the solicitor.

After Charmian had gone to lie down after lunch Mrs. Pettigrew came in to her.

Charmian opened her eyes. "I didn't hear you knock, Mabel," she said.

"No," said Mrs. Pettigrew. "You didn't."

"Always knock," said Charmian.

"Mrs. Anthony," said Mrs. Pettigrew, "is getting too forgetful to manage the cooking. She has left out the salt three days running, as you know. There was a caterpillar cooked in yesterday's greens. She put all that garlic in the sweetbread casserole, said she thought it was celery—well

I mean to say. She boiled Godfrey's egg hard this morning, he couldn't touch it."

"Keep an eye on her, Mabel. You have little else to do."

Mrs. Pettigrew's feelings—those which prompted every action—rose to her throat at this independent attitude which Charmian had been gradually accumulating all winter. Mrs. Pettigrew's breath, as she stood over Charmian's bed became short and agitated.

"Sit down, Mabel. You are out of breath," said Charmian.

Mrs. Pettigrew sat down. Charmian watched her, trying to sort out in her mind this new complaint about Mrs. Anthony, and what it could signify, apart from its plain meaning. Her thoughts drifted once more, for reassurance, to the nursing home in Surrey, in the same way that, as she knew, Jean Taylor's thoughts would, in the past, rest on her savings in the bank when from time to time her life with the Colstons had become too oppressive.

Mrs. Pettigrew's breathing was worse. She had been suddenly caught in a gust of resentment which had been stirring within her since Charmian's partial recovery. She felt a sense of great injustice at the evident power Charmian exerted over Godfrey—so strong that she did not seem conscious of it. It was a spell of her personality so mighty that, for fear of his miserable infidelities in Spain and Belgium with Lisa Brooke coming to Charmian's knowledge, he had been, so far, docile before all the threats and deprivations of the past winter. Mabel Pettigrew had only needed to indicate that she was in possession of the full correspondence between Lisa Brooke and Godfrey, dated 1902, 1903 and 1904, and his one immediate idea had been: Charmian must not know. Tell Eric, tell everyone. But keep it from Charmian.

Mrs. Pettigrew was aware that in this he was not displaying any special consideration for Charmian's feelings. That might have been endurable. The real reason was beyond her grasp, yet undeniably present. It was real enough to render Godfrey limp in her hands. What he seemed to fear was some superiority in Charmian and the loss of his pride before her. And, though Mabel Pettigrew indeed was doing better out of Godfrey than she had hoped, she sat in Charmian's bedroom and overwhelmingly resented the inexplicableness of Charmian's power.

"You seem to have a mild touch of asthma," Charmian remarked. "Better keep as still and quiet as possible and presently I will get Godfrey to ring the doctor."

Mrs. Pettigrew was thinking of that business scandal at Colston Breweries which had been hushed up at the time, the documents of which she now had in her keeping. Now, if Godfrey had been really frightened about her possible disclosure of these documents she would have understood him. But all he worried about were those letters between himself and Lisa Brooke. Charmian must not know. His pride before Charmian, Charmian, an old wreck like Charmian.

Charmian stretched her hand towards the bell-push by her bed. "Godfrey will ring for the doctor," she said.

"No, no, I'm better now," said Mrs. Pettigrew, gradually controlling her breath, for she had the self-discipline of a nun where business was concerned. "It was just a little turn. Mrs. Anthony is such a worry."

Charmian leaned back on her pillow and moved her hand wearily over her heart-shaped face. "Have you had asthma before, Mabel?"

"It is not asthma. It's just a little chest trouble." Mrs. Pettigrew's face was less alarmingly red. She breathed slowly and deeply after her ordeal, and lit a cigarette.

"You have great courage, Mabel," Charmian observed, "if only you would employ it to the proper ends. I envy your courage. I sometimes feel helpless without my friends around me. Very few of my friends come to see me now. It isn't their fault. Godfrey did not seem to want them after my stroke. When my friends were around me every day, what courage I had!"

"You would be better off in the home," said Mabel Pettigrew. "You know you would. Lots of company, your friends might even come and visit you sometimes."

"It's true I would prefer to be in the nursing home. However," said Charmian, "Godfrey needs me here."

"That's where you're wrong," said Mrs. Pettigrew.

Charmian wondered, once more, which of Godfrey's secrets the woman could have got hold of. The Colston Brewery affair? Or merely one or more of his numerous infidelities? Of course, one was always obliged to appear to know nothing where a man like Godfrey was concerned. His pride. It had been the only way to live reasonably with him. For a moment, she was tempted to go to Godfrey and say, "There is nothing you can tell me about your past life which would move me in the slightest. I know most of your supposed secrets, and what I do not know would still not surprise me."

But she did not possess the courage to do this. He might—he would certainly—turn on her. He would never forgive her for having played this game, for over fifty years, of knowing nothing while at the same time knowing everything, as one might be "not at home" while actually in the house. What new tyranny might he not exert to punish her knowledge?

And the simple idea of *facing* each other with such a statement between them was terrible. This should have been done years ago. And yet, it should not have been done. There was altogether too much candour in married life; it was an indelicate modern idea, and frequently led to upsets in a household, if not divorce. . . .

And she, too, had her pride to consider. Her mind munched over the humiliations she had received from Godfrey. Never had she won a little praise or recognition but she had paid for it by some bitter, petty, disruptive action of Godfrey's.

But I could sacrifice my pride, she thought, in order to release him. It is a matter of courage. The most I can do is to stay on here, at home with him. She envied Mrs. Pettigrew her courage.

Mrs. Pettigrew rose and came to stand by her bed.

"You're more of a hindrance to Godfrey here than you would be in a nursing home. It's ridiculous to say he needs you."

"I shall not go," said Charmian. "Now I think I must have my nap. What is the time?"

"I came," said Mrs. Pettigrew, "to tell you about Mrs. Anthony. She can't do the cooking any more, we shall all have stomach trouble. I will have to take over the meals. And besides, this cold supper she leaves for us at night is not satisfactory. It doesn't agree with me, going to bed on a cold supper. I will have to take over the cooking."

"That is very good of you," murmured Charmian, calculating meanwhile what was behind all this, since, with Mrs. Pettigrew, something always seemed to be behind her statements.

"Otherwise," said Mrs. Pettigrew, "one of us might be poisoned."

"Well, really!" said Charmian.

"*Poisoned,*" said Mrs. Pettigrew. "Poison is so easy. Think it over."

She left the room.

Charmian was frightened, and at the same time a long-latent faculty stirred in her mind to assess the cheap melodrama of Mrs. Pettigrew's words. But Charmian's fear predominated in the end, and, as she lay fearfully in her bed, she knew she would not put it past Mrs. Pettigrew to poison her once she took control of the food. A poisoning was not easy to accomplish, but still Mrs. Pettigrew might know of undetectable methods. Charmian thought on and on, and frightened herself more and more. Another woman, she thought, would be able to go to her husband and say, "Our housekeeper is threatening to poison me" —or to insist on an investigation by her friends, her son, the doctor. But Godfrey was craven, Eric was hostile, the doctor would attempt to soothe her down, assuming she had started to entertain those wild suspicions of the aged.

Then it is settled, Charmian thought. This is the point where my long, long duty to Godfrey comes to an end. I shall go to the nursing home.

The decision gave her a sense of latitude and relief. In the nursing home she could be a real person again, as she had been yesterday with Henry Mortimer, instead of a frightened invalid. She needed respect and attention. Perhaps she would have visitors. There, she could invite those whom she was prevented from seeing here at home through Godfrey's rudeness. The nursing home was not far from Stedrost. Perhaps Guy Leet would be driven over to see her. Guy Leet was amusing.

She heard the front door slam and then the slam of the car door. Mrs. Pettigrew's footsteps followed immediately, clicking towards the front door. Charmian heard her open the door and call, "Godfrey, I'm coming with you. Wait." But the car had already started and Godfrey was gone. Mrs. Pettigrew slammed the door shut once more and went to her room. A few seconds later she had descended the stairs and left the house.

Mrs. Pettigrew had informed Godfrey of her intention of accompanying him to his solicitor. When she found he had once given her the slip she felt pretty sure he had no intention of keeping his appointment with the lawyer. Within a few moments she had put on her hat and coat and marched up the road to find a taxi.

First of all she went to the bombed building off the King's Road. There, sure enough, was Godfrey's car.

There was, however, no sign of Godfrey. She ordered the taxi to drive round the block in a hope that she would catch Godfrey before he reached his destination, wherever that might be.

Godfrey, meanwhile, was on his way to Olive's flat, about seven minutes' walk for him at his fastest pace. He turned into Tite Street, stooping his head still more than his natural stoop, against a sudden shower of rain. He hoped Olive would have tea ready. He hoped Olive would not have any other visitors to-day, obliging him to enquire, in that foolish way, for the address of her grandfather. Olive would be in a listening mood, she was a good consoling listener. She would probably have heard from Eric. Godfrey wondered what she had heard from Eric. Olive had promised to write and tell Eric, in strictest confidence, about his difficulties with Mrs. Pettigrew. She had promised to appeal to Eric. Eric would no doubt be only too glad to be on good terms with his parents again. Eric had been a disappointment, but now was his chance to prove himself. Eric would put everything right, and no doubt Olive had heard from Eric.

He reached the area gate and pushed it open. There was an unusual amount of litter down in the area. The dust-bin was crammed full; old shoes, handbags and belts were sticking out beneath the lid. On the area pavement were scattered newspapers, tins, rusty kitchen utensils, empty bottles of numerous shapes, and a battered lamp-shade. Godfrey thought: Olive must be having a spring-clean, turning out all her things. Very wasteful and untidy. Always complaining of being hard up; no wonder.

No one answered his ring. He walked over to the barred window of Olive's front room and it was then he noticed the curtains had gone. He peered in. The room was quite bare. Must he not have come to the wrong house? He walked up the steps and looked carefully at the number. He walked down the steps again and peered once more into the empty room. Olive had definitely departed. And on realising this his first thought was to leave the vicinity of the house as quickly as possible. There was something mysterious about this. Godfrey could not stand anything mysterious. Olive might be involved in some scandal. She had said nothing, when he had seen her last week, about moving from her flat. As he walked away down Tite Street he feared more and more some swift, sudden scandal, and his one desire was to forget all knowledge of Olive.

He cut along the King's Road, bought an afternoon paper, and turned up the side street where his car was waiting. Before he reached it a taxi drew up beside him. Mrs. Pettigrew got out.

"Oh, there you are," she said.

He stood with the newspaper hanging from his hand while she paid the taxi, bewildered by guilt. This guilt was the main sensation Mrs. Pettigrew touched off in him. No thought, word or deed of his life had roused in him any feeling resembling the guilt he experienced as he stood waiting for Mrs. Pettigrew to pay the taxi and turn to ask him, "Where have you been?"

"Buying the paper," said Godfrey.

"Did you have to park your car here in order to walk down the road to buy the paper?"

"Wanted a walk," said Godfrey. "Bit stiff."

"You'll be late for your appointment. Hurry up. I told you to wait for me. Why did you go off without me?"

"I forgot," said Godfrey as he climbed into the car, "that you wanted to come. I was in a hurry to get to the lawyer's." She went round to the other side of the car and got in.

"You might have opened the door for me," she said.

Godfrey did not at first understand what she meant, for he had long since started to use his advanced years as an excuse to omit the mannerly conformities of his younger days, and he was now automatically rude in his gestures as if by long-earned right. He sensed some new frightful upheaval of his habits behind her words, as he drove off fitfully towards Sloane Square.

She lifted the paper and glanced at the front page.

"Ronald," she said. "Here's Ronald Sidebottome in the paper. His photo; he's got married. No, don't look. Watch where you're going, we'll have an accident. Mind out—there's the red light."

They were jerked forward roughly as Godfrey braked for the red light.

"Oh, do be careful," she said, "and a little more considerate."

He looked down at her lap where the paper was lying. Ronald's flabby face beamed up at him. He stood with Olive simpering on his arm, under the headline, "Widower, 79, weds girl, 24."

"Olive Mannering!" Godfrey let out.

"Oh, you know her?"

"Grand-daughter of my friend the poet," Godfrey said.

"The lights, Godfrey," said Mrs. Pettigrew in a tired tone.

He shot the car forward.

" 'Wealthy ex-stockbroker . . .' " Mrs. Pettigrew read out. "She knows what she's doing, all right. 'Miss Mannering . . . film extra and B.B.C. actress . . . now given up her flat in Tite Street, Chelsea . . .' " The jig-saw began to piece itself together in Mrs. Pettigrew's mind. As heart is said to speak unto heart, Mrs. Pettigrew looked at Olive's photograph and understood where Godfrey had been wont to go on those afternoons when he had parked his car outside the bombed building.

"Of course, Godfrey, this will be a blow to you," she said.

He thought: God, she knows everything. He went up to his solicitor's offices like a lamb, while Mrs. Pettigrew waited in the car below. He did not even attempt to circumvent her wishes, as he had half-hoped to do when finally forced to the alteration of his will. He did not now even think of the idea he had previously dabbled with, of confiding the facts to his lawyer. Mabel Pettigrew knew everything. She could tell Charmian everything. He instructed a new will to be drawn up leaving the minimum required by law to his son, and the bulk to Mrs. Pettigrew, and even most of Charmian's share, should she outlive him, in trust for Mrs. Pettigrew.

"Now," said the solicitor. "This might take some time to prepare, of course."

"It must be done right away," said Godfrey.

"Would you not like some time, Mr. Colston, to think it over? Mrs. Pettigrew is your housekeeper?"

"It must be done right away," said Godfrey. "No delay, if you please."

"Disgusting," said Godfrey later that evening to Charmian. "A man going on eighty marrying a girl of twenty-four. Absolutely disgusting. And he's deaf as a post."

"Godfrey," she said, "I am going to the nursing home on Sunday morning. I have made arrangements with the doctor and the bank. Universal Aunts are coming tomorrow to pack my things. Janet Sidebottome will accompany me. I do not wish to put you out, Godfrey. It might distress you to take me yourself. I am afraid I simply can't stand these anonymous telephone calls any longer. They will bring me speedily to my grave. I must be protected from the sight of the telephone. I have spoken to Lettie, and she approves my decision. Mrs. Pettigrew thinks, too, it will be the best course—don't you, Mabel? Everyone is agreed. I must say, I feel most sad. However, it had to be eventually. You yourself have often said—"

"But you don't mind the telephone calls!" he shouted. "You don't care about them at all."

"Oh yes, I do, I do. I can't put up with them any longer."

"She does mind them," said Mrs. Pettigrew.

"But you don't need to answer the phone," he shouted.

"Oh but every time the telephone rings I feel it must be *him*." Charmian gave a little shudder.

"She feels so bad about the telephone," said Mrs. Pettigrew.

He knew he could not refute their words.

Chapter Thirteen

"What surprised me, I must confess," Alec Warner said to Miss Taylor, "was that, for a moment or two, I felt positively jealous. Olive, of course, was a friendly type of girl, and most conscientious in giving me all the information she could gather. I shall miss her. But the curious thing was this pang, this envy of Ronald, my first reaction to the news. Not that Olive, at any time, would have been my type."

"Did you make a note of your reaction?"

"Oh, I made a note."

I bet he did, thought Miss Taylor.

"Oh, I made a note. I always record these surprise deviations from my High-Churchmanship."

His "High-Churchmanship" was a figure of speech he had adopted from Jean Taylor when, at some buoyant time past, she had applied it to him, merely on account of the two occasions when he had darkened the doors of a church, to observe, with awe and curiosity, a vicar of his acquaintance conducting the service of evensong all by himself in the empty building; Alec's awe and curiosity being directed exclusively towards the human specimen with his prayer book and splendid persistence in vital habits.

"Granny Green has gone," said Miss Taylor.

"Ah yes, I noticed a stranger occupying her bed. Now what was Granny Green?"

"Arterio-sclerosis. It affected her heart in the end."

"Yes, well, it is said we are all as old as our arteries. Did she make a good death?"

"I don't know."

"You were asleep at the time," he said.

"No, I was awake. There was a certain amount of fuss."

"She didn't have a peaceful end?"

"No, not peaceful for us."

"I always like to know," he said, "whether a death is a good or bad one. Do keep a look out."

For a moment she utterly hated him. "A good death," she said, "doesn't reside in the dignity of bearing but in the disposition of the soul."

Suddenly he hated her. "Prove it," he said.

"Disprove it," she said wearily.

"I'm afraid," he said, "I've forgotten to ask how you are keeping. How are you keeping, Jean?"

"A little stronger, but the cataract is a trouble."

"Charmian is gone to the nursing home in Surrey at last. Would you not like to join her there?"

"Godfrey is left alone with Mrs. Pettigrew, then."

"You would like to be with Charmian, surely."

"No," she said.

He looked round the ward and up to the noisy end. There the senile cases were grouped round the television and so were less noisy than usual, but still emitting, from time to time, a variety of dental and guttural sounds and sometimes a whole, well-intentioned speech. Those who were mobile would occasionally leave their chairs and wander up the ward, waving or talking to the bedridden. One tall patient poured herself a beaker of water and began to raise it to her lips, but forgetting the purpose before the act was accomplished, poured the water into another jug; then she turned the beaker upside down on her head so that a little water, left in the beaker, splashed over her forehead. She seemed pleased with this feat. On the whole, the geriatrics were keen on putting objects on their heads.

"Interesting," said Alec. "The interesting thing is, senility is somewhat different from insanity. The actions of these people, for instance, differ in many particulars from those of the aged people whom I visit at St. Aubrey's Home in Folkestone. There, some of the patients have been mad most of their lives. In some ways they are more coherent, much more methodical than those who merely turn strange in their old age. The really mad old people have had more practice in irrational behavior, of course. But all this," said Alec, "cannot be of much interest to you. Unless one is interested in gerontology, I cannot see that their company, day and night, can be pleasant to you."

"Perhaps I'm a gerontologist at heart. They are harmless. I don't mind them, now. Alec, I am thinking of poor Godfrey Colston. What can have possessed Charmian to go away just when her health was improving?"

"The anonymous telephone calls were worrying her, she said."

"Oh no. Mrs. Pettigrew must have forced her to go. And Mrs. Pettigrew," said Miss Taylor, "will most certainly make Godfrey's remaining years a misery."

He reached for his hat. "Think over," he said, "the idea of joining Charmian in the nursing home. It would so please me if you would."

"Now Alec, I can't leave my old friends. Miss Valvona, Miss Duncan—"

"And this?" He nodded towards the senile group.

"That is our memento mori. Like your telephone calls."

"Goodbye then, Jean."

"Oh Alec, I wish you wouldn't leave just yet. I have something important to say, if you will just sit still for a moment and let me get my thoughts in order."

He sat still. She leaned back on her pillow, removed

her glasses, and dabbed lightly with her handkerchief at one eye which was inflamed. She replaced her glasses.

"I shall have to think," she said. "It involves a question of dates. I have them in my memory but I shall have to think for a few minutes. While you are waiting you may care to speak to the new patient in Granny Green's bed. Her name is Mrs. Bean. She is ninety-nine and will be a hundred in September."

He went to speak to Mrs. Bean, tiny among the pillows, her small toothless mouth open like an "O," her skin stretched thin and white over her bones, her huge eye-sockets and eyes in a fixed infant-like stare, and her sparse white hair short and straggling over her brow. Her head nodded faintly and continuously. If she had not been in a female ward, Alec thought, one might not have been sure whether she was a very old man or a woman. She reminded him of one of his mental patients at Folkestone, an old man who, since 1918, had believed he was God. Alec spoke to Mrs. Bean and received a civil and coherent answer which came, as it seemed, from a primitive reed instrument in her breast-bone, so thin and high did she breathe, in and out, when answering him.

He stepped over to Miss Valvona, paid his respects, and heard from her his horoscope for the day. He nodded to Mrs. Reewes-Duncan, and waved to various other occupants of the ward familiar to him. One of the geriatric set came and shook hands with him and said she was going to the bank, and, having departed from the ward, was escorted back by a nurse who said to her, "Now you've been to the bank."

Alec carefully watched the patient's happy progress back to the geriatric end, reflected on the frequency with which the senile babble about the bank, and returned to Jean Taylor who said:

"You must inform Godfrey Colston that Charmian was unfaithful to him repeatedly from the year after her marriage. That is starting in the summer of 1902 when Charmian had a villa on Lake Geneva, and throughout that year, when Charmian used often to visit the man in his flat in Hyde Park Gate. And this went on throughout 1903 and 1904 and also, I recall, when Charmian was up in Perthshire in the autumn—Godfrey could not leave London at the time. There were also occasions at Biarritz and Torquay. Have you got that, Alec? Her lover was Guy Leet. She continued to see him at his flat in Hyde Park Gate through most of 1905—up to September. Listen carefully, Alec, you are to give Godfrey Colston all the facts. Guy Leet. So she gave him up in the September of 1907, I well remember, I was with them in the Dolomites, and Charmian became ill then. You must remember Guy is ten years younger than Charmian. Then in 1926 the affair began again, and it went on for about eighteen months. That was about the time I met you, Alec. Guy wanted her to leave Godfrey, and I know she thought of doing so quite often. But then she knew Guy had so many other women—Lisa Brooke, of course, and so on. Charmian couldn't really trust Guy. Charmian missed him, he did so amuse her. After that she entered the Church. Now I want you to give these facts to Godfrey. He has never suspected Charmian, she managed everything so well. Have you got a pencil on you, Alec? Better write it down. First occasion, 1902—"

"You know, Jean," he said, "this might be serious for poor Godfrey and Charmian. I mean, I can't think you really want to betray Charmian after all those years."

"I don't want to," she said, "but I will, Alec."

"Godfrey probably knows already," he said.

"The only people who know about this are Charmian, Guy, and myself. Lisa Brooke knew, and in fact she blackmailed Charmian quite cruelly. That was when Charmian had her nervous breakdown. And in fact the main reason Guy married Lisa was to keep her quiet, and save Charmian from the threat of scandal. It was never a proper marriage, but, however, as I say, Guy did marry Lisa for Charmian's sake. I will say that for him. Of course, Guy Leet did have charm."

"He still has charm," said Alec.

"Has he? Well, I don't doubt it. Now, Alec, write this down, will you?"

"Jean, you would regret it."

"Alec, if you won't give Godfrey this information I shall have to ask Dame Lettie to do so. She would make the matter far more unpleasant for Charmian. I see it is necessary that Godfrey Colston should stop being morally afraid of Charmian—at least it is worth trying. I think, if he knows of Charmian's infidelity he won't fear any disclosures about his. Let him go and gloat over Charmian. Let him—"

"Charmian will be shocked. She trusts you." He put the case for the opposition, but she knew he was stirred and excited by her suggestion. He had never, in the past, hesitated to make mischief if it served his curiosity: now he could serve her ends.

"There is a time for loyalty and a time when loyalty comes to an end. Charmian should know that by now," she said.

He looked at her curiously as if to find in her face something that he had previously overlooked, some latent jealousy.

"The more religious people are, the more perplexing I find them. And I think Charmian would be hurt by your action."

"Charmian herself is a religious woman."

"No, only a woman with a religion." He had always found it odd that Miss Taylor, having entered the Church only to please Charmian, should have become the more addicted of the two.

He made notes of the information Miss Taylor gave to

him. "Make it clear," she said, "that this is a message from me. If my hands were in use I would write to him myself. Tell him from me he has nothing to fear from Mrs. Pettigrew. Poor old man."

"Were you ever jealous of Charmian?" he said.

"Of course I was," she said, "from time to time."

Alec was wondering as he wrote down the details of Charmian's love affair, if Godfrey Colston would be agreeable to taking his pulse and temperature before and after the telling. On the whole, he thought not. Guy Leet had been obliging in this respect, but then Guy was a sport. Still, one might try.

"You know, Taylor," said Dame Lettie, "I do not feel I can continue to visit you. These creatures are too disturbing, and now that I am not getting my proper sleep my nerves are not up to these decrepit women here. One wonders, really, what is the purpose of keeping them alive at the country's expense."

"For my part," said Miss Taylor, "I would be glad to be let die in peace. But the doctors would be horrified to hear me say it. They are so proud of their new drugs and new methods of treatment—there is always something new. I sometimes fear, at the present rate of discovery, I shall never die."

Dame Lettie considered this statement, uncertain whether it was frivolous or not. She shifted bulkily in her chair and considered the statement with a frown and a downward droop of her facial folds.

Miss Taylor supplied obligingly: "Of course the principle of keeping people alive is always a good one."

Dame Lettie glanced along the ward at the geriatrics who were, at that moment, fairly docile. One old lady sat up in her cot singing a song or something; a few were being visited by relatives who spoke little but for the most part simply sat out the visiting time with their feeble forebears, occasionally breaking the silence with some piece of family news, spoken loudly into the half-comprehending faces, and accepting with blank calm the response, whether this were a cluck or a crow, or something more substantial. The rest of the geriatric patients were grouped at the television corner, watching and commenting. Really, there was nothing one could complain of in them.

But Lettie had been, in any case, jittery beyond the usual when she arrived. She had not answered Miss Taylor's greeting, but had scraped the bedside chair closer to Miss Taylor and started talking immediately.

"Taylor, we all went to see Mortimer. It was utterly futile—"

"Oh, yes, Mr. Warner told me yesterday—"

"Quite useless. Mortimer is not to be trusted. The police are, of course, shielding him. He must have accomplices—one of them is apparently a young man, another a middle-aged man with a lisp, and then there is a foreigner, and also—"

"Chief Inspector Mortimer," said Miss Taylor, "always used to seem to me rather sane."

"Sane, of course he's sane. I am not saying he isn't sane. I made the great mistake, Taylor, of letting him know I had remembered him in my will. He always appeared to be so helpful on the committees, so considerate. But I see now, he has been a schemer. He did not expect me to live so long, and he is using these methods to frighten me to death. Of course I have now taken him out of my will, and I took steps to make this fact known to him, hoping his persecution would then cease. But now, in his rage, he has intensified his efforts. The others who receive the anonymous calls are merely being used as a blind, a cover, you see, Taylor, a blind. And Eric, I believe, is working in with him. I have written to Eric, but have received no reply, which alone is suspicious. I am their main objective and victim. Now, a further development. A few weeks ago, you remember I arranged to have my telephone disconnected."

"Oh yes," said Miss Taylor, closing her eyes to rest them.

"Well, shortly after that, as I was going to bed, I could swear I heard a noise at my bedroom window. As you know, my window looks out on the . . ."

Dame Lettie had, in the past few weeks, got into the habit of searching the house every night before going to bed. One could not be too careful. She searched the house from top to bottom, behind sofas, in cupboards, under beds. And even then there were creaks and unaccountable noises springing up all over the place. This nightly search of the house and the garden took three-quarters of an hour, by the end of which Dame Lettie was in no condition to deal with her maid's hysterics. After a week of this routine Gwen had declared the house to be haunted and Dame Lettie to be a maniac, and had left.

Thus, Dame Lettie was not in the mood for the geriatrics when she visited Miss Taylor in the Maud Long Ward.

"I suppose," ventured Miss Taylor, "you have informed the police of your suspicions. If someone is trying to get into the house, surely the police—"

"The police," Dame Lettie explained with long-tried emphasis, "are shielding Mortimer and his accomplices. The police always stick together. Eric is in with them. They are all in it together."

"Perhaps a little rest in a country nursing home would do you good. All this must be very exhausting."

"Not me," said Dame Lettie. "Oh no, Taylor, no nursing home for me while I have my faculties and am able to get about on my feet. I am looking for another maid. An older woman. They are so difficult to come by, they all want their television." She looked over to the senile patients gathered round their television receiver.

"Such an expense to the country. An abominable invention."

"Really, in cases like theirs, it is an entirely suitable invention. It does hold their attention."

"Taylor, I cannot come here again. It is too distressing."

"Go away for a holiday, Dame Lettie. Forget about the house and the phone calls."

"Even the private detective whom I employed is in league with Mortimer. Mortimer is behind it all. Eric is . . ."

Miss Taylor dabbed her sore eye under her glasses. She wanted to close her eyes, and longed for the bell to ring which marked the end of the visiting hour.

"Mortimer . . . Mortimer . . . Eric," Dame Lettie was going on. Miss Taylor felt reckless.

"In my belief," she said, "the author of the anonymous telephone calls is Death himself, as you might say. I don't see, Dame Lettie, what you can do about it. If you don't remember Death, Death reminds you to do so. And if you can't cope with the facts the next best thing is to go away for a holiday."

"You have taken leave of your senses, Taylor," said Dame Lettie, "and I can do no more for you." She stopped at the outer office and, demanding to speak to the ward sister, registered her opinion that Miss Taylor was off her head and should be watched.

When Gwen had left Dame Lettie's employment she quite understandably told her boy friend all about the nightly goings-on, how the mad Dame would go round the house, poking into all the cupboards and corners, and the garden, poking into the shrubberies with an electric torch, no wonder her eyesight was failing.

"And she wouldn't let me tell the police," said Gwen. "She doesn't trust the police. No wonder, they'd have laughed at her. Oh, but it gave me the creeps because when you're looking for noises, you keep hearing them all over the house and you think you see shapes in the darkness, and half the time it was herself I bumped into in the garden. Oh, but that house is just about haunted. I couldn't stand it a minute longer."

Gwen's boy friend thought it a good story and recounted it at his work which was in a builder's yard.

"My girl was in with an old girl, some dame or countess or other up Hampstead way . . . went round the place every night . . . kept hearing burglars . . . wouldn't get the police . . . My girl walked out on her a week past, too much of it. . . ."

"There's some cranky ones going about," commented one of his friends, "I'll tell you. I remember during the war when I was batman to a colonel, he . . ."

So it was that a labourer, new to the yard, picked up Gwen's story—a youth who would not have considered himself a criminal type, but who knew a window cleaner who would give two or perhaps three pounds an item for likely information. But you had to have an address.

"Where'd you say this countess was living?" he said to Gwen's boy. "I know all up Hampstead and round the Heath."

Gwen's boy said, "Oh, this is a posh part, Hackleton Rise. My girl says the old woman'll be carted off looney in the end. She's one of them. Did you see in the papers about the phone-call hoax? She's cut off her phone now . . ."

The young labourer took his information to the window cleaner, who did not pay him immediately. "I got to check the address with my contact."

The window cleaner himself never actually touched a job like this, but there was money in information. In a few days' time his contact expressed himself satisfied, and paid over ten pounds, remarking that the old girl in question wasn't a countess after all. The window cleaner duly paid a small share to the young labourer remarking that the information was a bit faulty, and that he'd better not be leaky with his mouth the next few days.

So it came about that Dame Lettie's house and nocturnal searching fell under scrutiny.

On the day of her last visit to Miss Taylor she returned to Hampstead by taxi shortly after five. She called in at the employment agency to see if they had found her a woman yet, a middle-aged woman, clean with good references, to live in. No, they had found no one yet, Dame Lettie, but they were keeping their eyes open. She walked the rest of the way home.

Gloomily she made a pot of tea and drank a cup standing in the kitchen. She then puffed her way into her study and started writing a letter to Eric. Her fountain-pen ran out of ink. She refilled it and continued,

> . . . I am thinking only of your poor mother put away in a home, and your poor old father who has done so much for you, and who is rapidly failing in health, when I demand that at least you should write and explain your silence. There has been bitterness between your parents and yourself, I know. But the time is come, surely, in their declining years, for you to make what amends you can. Your father was telling me only the other day, that, for his part, he is willing to let bygones be bygones. In fact, he asked me to write to you in this vein.

She stopped and looked out the window. An unfamiliar car had pulled up at the house opposite. Someone visiting the Dillingers, apparently, not knowing the Dillingers were away. She began to feel chilly and got up to draw the curtain. A man was sitting waiting in the car. As she drew the curtains, he drove off. She returned to her desk and continued,

Do not suppose I am not aware of your activities in London and your attempts to frighten me. Do not suppose I am in the least alarmed.

She scored these last sentences through with her pen. That was not what she had meant to write. She had, at first, thought of writing in this manner, but her second thoughts, she now recalled, had decided her to write something more in the nature of an appeal. One had to employ cunning with a man like Eric. She took a fresh sheet and began again, stopping once to look over her shoulder at a potential noise.

I am thinking only of your poor mother put away in a home, and your poor old father, enfeebled and rapidly failing in health, when I . . .

She finished the letter, addressed and sealed it, and called Gwen to catch the six o'clock post. Then she remembered Gwen had left.

Dame Lettie laid the letter helplessly on the hall table and pulled herself together so far as to think of supper and to switch on the news.

She prepared her supper of steamed fish, ate it and washed up. She listened to the wireless till half-past nine. Then she turned it off and went into the hall where she stood for about five minutes, listening. Eventually, various sounds took place, coming successively from the kitchen quarters, the dining-room on her right, and upstairs.

She spent the next forty-five minutes in a thorough search of the house and the garden, front and back. Then she locked and bolted the front door and the back door. She locked every room and took away the keys. Finally she climbed slowly up to bed, stopping every few steps to regain her breath and to listen. Certainly, there was somebody on the roof.

She locked her bedroom door behind her and tilted a chair under the door knob. Certainly, there was someone down there in the garden. She must get in touch with the Member tomorrow. He had not replied to her previous letter which she had posted on Monday, or was it Tuesday? Well, there had been time for a reply. Corruption in the police force was a serious matter. There would have to be a question in the House. One was entitled to one's protection. She put her hand out to feel the heavy walking-stick securely propped by her bed. She fell asleep at last. She woke suddenly with the noise in her ears, and after all, was amazed by the reality of this.

She switched on the light. It was five past two. A man was standing over by her dressing-table, the drawers of which were open and disarranged. He had turned round to face her. Her bedroom door was open. There was a light in the passage and she heard someone else padding along it. She screamed, grabbed her stick, and was attempting to rise from her bed when a man's voice from the passage outside said, "That's enough, let's go." The man by the dressing-table hesitated nervily for a moment, then swiftly he was by Lettie's side. She opened wide her mouth and her yellow and brown eyes. He wrenched the stick from the old woman's hand and, with the blunt end of it, battered her to death. It was her eighty-first year.

Chapter Fourteen

Four days passed before the milkman reported an accumulation of four pints of milk on Dame Lettie's doorstep, and the police entered her house to find the body, half in, half out of her bed.

Meanwhile Godfrey did not wonder, even vaguely, why he had not heard from Lettie. Now that her telephone was disconnected he seldom heard from her. In any case, he had other things to think about that morning. Alec Warner had been to see him with that extraordinary disturbing, impudent, yet life-giving message from Taylor. He had, of course, ordered Warner out of the house. Alec had seemed to expect this and had departed with easy promptitude to Godfrey's "Get out," like an actor who had rehearsed the part. He had, however, left a slip of paper behind him, bearing a series of dates and place-names. Godfrey examined the document and felt unaccountably healthier than he had been for some months. He went out and bought himself a whisky and soda while he decided what to do. And, over his drink, he despised Guy Leet yet liked the thought of him, since he was associated with his new sense of well-being. He had another whisky, and chuckled to himself to think of Guy bent double over his two sticks. An ugly fellow; always had been, the little rotter.

Guy Leet sat in his room at the Old Stable, Stedrost, Surrey, laboriously writing his memoirs which were being

published by instalments in a magazine. The laborious-
ness of the task resided in the physical, not the mental
effort. His fingers worked slowly, clutched round the
large barrel of his fountain-pen. His fingers were good
for perhaps another year—if you could call these twisted,
knobble-knuckled members good. He glanced reproach-
fully at them from time to time—perhaps good for another
year, depending on the severity of the intervening winter.
How primitive, Guy thought, life becomes in old age,
when one may be surrounded by familiar comforts and yet
more vulnerable to the action of nature than any young
explorer at the Pole. And how simply the physical laws
assert themselves, frustrating all one's purposes. Guy
suffered from an internal disorder of the knee-joints which
caused one leg to collapse across the other whenever he
put his weight on it. But although he frequently remarked, "The law of gravity, the beast," he was actually
quite cheerful most of the time. He also suffered from a
muscular rheumatism of the neck which caused his head
to be perpetually thrust forward and askew. However, he
adapted his eyesight and body as best he could to these
defects, looking at everything sideways and getting about
with the aid of his servant and his car, or on two sticks. He
had in his service a pious, soft-spoken, tip-toeing un-
married middle-aged Irishman for whom Guy felt much
affection, and whom he called Tony to his face and Creep-
ing Jesus behind his back.

Tony came in with his morning coffee and the mail,
which always arrived late. Tony placed two letters beside
the paper-knife. He placed the coffee before Guy. He
stroked the fronts of his trousers, wriggled and beamed.
He was doing a Perpetual Novena for Guy's conversion,
even though Guy had told him, "The more you pray for
me, Tony, the more I'm a hardened sinner. Or would be,
if I had half a chance."

He opened the larger envelope. Proofs of the latest installment of his memoirs. "Here, Tony," he said, "check these proofs."

"Ah, ye know I can't read without me glasses."

"That's a euphemism, Tony." For Tony's reading capacity was not too good, though he managed when necessary by following each word with his finger.

"Indeed, sir, 'tis a pity." Tony disappeared.

Guy opened the other letter and gave a smile which might have appeared sinister to one who did not realise that this was only another consequence of his neck being twisted. The letter was from Alec Warner.

DEAR GUY,

I'm afraid I sent Percy Mannering the last instalment of your *memoirs*. He would have seen it, in any case. I'm afraid he is a trifle upset about your further reference to Dowson.

Mannering in replying to thank me for sending him the article, tells me he is coming down to see you, no doubt to talk things over. I hope he will not prove too difficult and that you will make all allowances.

Now, dear fellow, you will, I know, assist me by taking the old fellow's pulse and temperature as soon as it can conveniently be done after he has discussed the article with you. Preferably, of course, *during* the discussion, but this may prove difficult. Any further observations as to his colour, speech (clarity of, etc.) and general bearing *during* the little discussion will be most welcome, as you know.

Mannering will be with you tomorrow, i.e. the day on which you will, I expect, receive this letter—at about 3.40 p.m. I have supplied him with train times and all necessary directions.

My dear Fellow,

I am, most gratefully,

Alec Warner

Guy put the letter back into its envelope. He telephoned to the nursing home where Charmian was now resident and asked if he might call and see her that afternoon, and was informed, after the nurse had been to make enquiries, that he might. He then told Tony to have the car ready at three-fifteen.

He had intended to see Charmian, in any case. And to-day was warm and bright, though clouds came over at intervals. He held no resentment against Alec Warner. The chap was a born mischief-maker; but he didn't know it, that was the saving grace. He was sorry poor Percy would have to undergo the journey for nothing that afternoon.

When he left at a quarter past three he left a message on the door of his Old Stable, "Away for a few days." Quite improbable, it sounded, but Percy would have to take it or leave it.

" 'Tis a lie," commented Tony, sliding into the car to drive his master off.

Charmian liked her new room. It was large and furnished with bright old-fashioned chintzes. It reminded her of her headmistress's room at school in those times when the days were always, somehow, sunny, and everyone seemed to love each other. She had been quite eighteen years of age before she had realised that everyone did not love each other; this was a fact which she had always found it difficult to convey to others. "But surely, Charmian, you must have come across spitefulness and hatred before you were eighteen?"

"Only in retrospect," she would reply, "did I discern discord in people's actions. At the time, all seemed harmony. Everyone loved each other."

Some said she was colouring the past with the rosy glow of nostalgia. But she plainly remembered her shock when, at the age of eighteen, she became conscious of evil—a trifling occasion; her sister had said something detrimental about her—but it was only then that Charmian discovered the reality of words like "sin" and "calumny" which she had known, as words, for as long as she could remember.

The window of her room looked out on a lawn in the centre of which stood a great elm. She could sit at her window and watch the other patients walking in the grounds, and they might have been the girls at her old school sauntering at their recreation period, and she with her headmistress taking tea by the window.

"Everything," she said to Guy some time after he had made his difficult way across the room, "has an innocent air in this place. I feel almost free from Original Sin."

"How dull for you, dear," said Guy.

"It's an illusion, of course."

A young nurse brought in tea and placed it between them. Guy winked at her. The nurse winked back, and left them.

"Behave yourself, Guy."

"And how," he said, "did you leave Godfrey?"

"Oh, he was most depressed. These anonymous telephone calls worry him." She gestured towards her white telephone receiver. The civil young man had vaguely assumed in her mind the shape of a telephone receiver. At home he had been black; here he was white. "Does he worry you, Guy?"

"Me? No. I don't mind a bit of fun."

"They worry Godfrey. It is surprising how variously people react to the same thing."

"Personally," said Guy, "I tell the young fellow to go to hell.

"Well, he vexed Godfrey. And then we have an unsuitable housekeeper. She also worries him. Godfrey has a lot of worries. You would see a change in him, Guy. He is failing."

"Doesn't like this revival of your books?"

"Guy, I don't like talking against Godfrey, you know. But, between ourselves, he *is* rather jealous. At his age, one would have thought he had no more room for these feelings, somehow. But there it is. He was so rude, Guy, to a young critic who came to see me."

"Fellow has never understood you," said Guy. "But still I perceive you have a slight sense of guilt concerning him."

"Guilt? Oh no, Guy. As I was saying, I feel unusually innocent in this place."

"Sometimes," he said, "a sense of guilt takes a self-righteous turn. I see no cause for you to feel either in the right or in the wrong where Godfrey's concerned."

"I have regular visits from a priest," she said, "and if I want moral advice, Guy, I shall consult him."

"Oh quite, quite." Guy placed his gnarled hand on her lap; he was afraid he was forgetting how to handle women.

"And then," said Charmian, "you know he has estranged Eric. It is really Godfrey's fault, Guy. I do not like to say these things, and of course Eric was a disappointment, but I can't help feeling Godfrey's attitude—"

"Eric," said Guy, "is a man of fifty-five."

"Fifty-seven," said Charmian, "next month."

"Fifty-seven," said Guy. "And he has had time to acquire a sense of responsibility."

"That," sighed Charmian, "Eric has never possessed. But I did think at one time he might have been a painter. I never had much hope for his writing, but his paintings—he did seem to have talent. At least, to me. But Godfrey was so mean about money, and Godfrey—"

"If I remember," said Guy, "it was not until Eric was past forty-five that Godfrey refused to give him any more money."

"And then Lettie," said Charmian, "has been so cruel about her wills. Always promising Eric the earth, and then retracting her promises. I don't know why she doesn't do something for Eric while she is still alive."

"Do you think," said Guy, "that money would make Eric any less spiteful?"

"Well, no," said Charmian, "I don't. I have been sending Eric sums of money for some years, secretly, through Mrs. Anthony who is our daily woman. But he is still spiteful. Of course he disapproves of my books."

"They are beautiful books," said Guy.

"Eric doesn't approve the style. I'm afraid Godfrey has never handled Eric tactfully, that is the trouble."

"Beautiful," said Guy. "I have just been re-reading *The Seventh Child*. I love particularly that scene at the end with Edna in her mackintosh standing at the cliff's edge on that Hebridean coast being drenched by the spray, and her hair blown about her face. And then turning to find Karl by her side. One thing about your lovers, Charmian, they never required any preliminary discussions. They simply looked at each other and *knew*."

"That," said Charmian, "is one of the things Eric cannot stand."

"Eric is a realist. He has no period-sense, no charity."

"Oh, my dear Guy, do you think these new young men read my books from charity?"

"Not from indulgence and kindness. But charity elevates the mind and governs the inward eye. If a valuable work of art is rediscovered after it has gone out of fashion, that is due to some charity in the discoverer, I believe. But I say, without a period-sense as well, no one can appreciate your books."

"Eric has no charity," she said.

"Well, perhaps it is just that he is middle-aged. The really young are so much pleasanter," said Guy.

She was not listening. "He is like Godfrey in so many ways," she said, "I can't help remembering how much I had to shut my eyes to in Godfrey. Lipstick on his hand-kerchiefs—"

"Stop feeling guilty about Godfrey," Guy said. He had expected a livelier meeting with Charmian. He had never known Charmian to complain so much. He wished he had not enquired after Godfrey in the first place. Her words depressed him. They were like spilt sugar; however much you swept it up some grains would keep grinding under your feet.

"About your novels," he said. "The plots are so well-laid. For instance in *The Seventh Child,* although of course one feels that Edna will never marry Gridsworthy, you have this tension between Anthony Garland and Colonel Yeoville, and until of course their relationships to Gabrielle are revealed, there is every likelihood that Edna will marry one or the other. And yet, of course, all along one is aware of a kind of *secret life* within Edna, especially at that moment when she is alone in the garden at Neuflette, and then comes unexpectedly upon Karl and Gabrielle. And then one feels sure she will marry Gridsworthy after all, merely for his kindness. And really, right up to the last page one does not know Karl's true feelings. Or rather, one knows them—but does *he* know them? I must admit, although I remembered the story well, I felt the same enormous sense of relief, when I read it again the other day, that Edna did not throw herself over the cliff. The suspense, the plot alone, quite apart from the prose, are superb."

"And yet," said Charmian, smiling up at the sky through the window, "when I was halfway through writing a novel I always got into a muddle and didn't know where it was leading me."

Guy thought: She is going to say—dear Charmian—she is going to say, "The characters seemed to take on a life of their own."

"The characters," said Charmian, "seemed to take control of my pen after a while. But at first I always got into a tangle. I used to say to myself,

> 'Oh what a tangled web we weave
> When first we practise to deceive!'

Because," she said, "the art of fiction is very like the practise of deception."

"And in life," he said, "is the practise of deception in life an art too?"

"In life," she said, "everything is different. Everything is in the Providence of God. When I think of my own life . . . Godfrey . . ."

Guy wished he had not introduced the question of life, but had continued discussing her novels. Charmian was upset about Godfrey, that was plain.

"Godfrey has not been to visit me yet. He is to come next week. If he is able. But he is failing. You see, Guy, he is his own worst enemy. He . . ."

How banal and boring, Guy thought, do the most interesting people become when they are touched by a little bit of guilt.

He left at five. Charmian watched him from the window being helped into his car. She was vexed with herself for going on so much about Godfrey. Guy had never been interested in her domestic affairs. He was such an amusing companion. The room, with its chintzes, felt empty.

Guy waved out of his car window, a stiff, difficult wave. It was only then that Charmian noticed the other car which had drawn up while Guy had been helped into his seat. Charmian peered down; it looked like Godfrey's car. It was, and Godfrey was climbing out, in his jerky way. She supposed he had come on an impulse to escape Mrs. Pettigrew. If only he could go to live in a quiet private hotel. But as he walked across the path, she noticed he looked astonishingly bright and healthy. She felt rather tired.

Guy Leet considered, as he was driven home, whether in fact he was enjoying that sense of calm and freedom that is supposed to accompany old age or whether he was not. Yesterday he had been an old, serene man. To-day he felt younger and less peaceful. How could one know at any particular moment what one's old age finally amounted to? On the whole, he thought, he must be undergoing the experience of calm and freedom, although it was not like anything he would have anticipated. He was, perhaps, comparatively untroubled and detached, mainly because he became so easily exhausted. He was amazed at Charmian's apparent energy—and she ten years his senior. He supposed he must be a dear old thing. He was fortunate in possessing all his material needs, and now that Lisa's will was being proved, he might possibly spend the winter in a really warm climate. And he had earned Lisa's money. And he bore no grudge against Charmian for her ingratitude. Not many men would have married Lisa simply to keep her quiet for Charmian's sake. Not many would have endured the secrecy of such a marriage, a mere legal bond necessary to Lisa's full sensual enjovment of her many perversions. "I've got to be married," she would say in that hoarse voice, "my dear, I don't want the man near me, but I've got to know I'm married or I can't enjoy myself."

Foolishly, they had exchanged letters on the subject, which might have upset his claim on Lisa's money. He did not think Tempest's suit would have succeeded, but it would have been unpleasant. But that eventuality had come to nothing. He would get Lisa's money; he had earned it. He had given satisfaction to Lisa and safety to Charmian.

He doubted if Charmian ever thought with gratitude of his action. Still, he adored Charmian. She had been wonderful, even when he had met her a year ago at a time when her mind was failing. Now that she was so greatly improved, what a pity she had this Godfrey trouble on her mind. However, he adored Charmian for what she had been and what she still really was. And he had earned Lisa's money. Trinidad might be delightful next winter. Or Barbados. He must write for some information.

When they drew up at the Old Stable Percy Mannering appeared out of the back garden and approached the car waving a magazine in the direction of the front door where Guy's message was pinned up.

"Away for a few days," shouted Percy.

"I have just returned," said Guy. "Tony will give me a hand, and then we will go indoors for a drink. Meanwhile let us not alarm the lilies of the field."

"Away for a few days," shouted Percy, "my foot."

Tony trotted round the car and took Guy by the arms.

"I've been waiting," shouted Percy, "for you."

Guy, as he was helped to his feet, was trying to recall what exactly he had written about Ernest Dowson in the latest published instalment of his memoirs which so enraged Percy. Guy was not a moment inside the door before he found out, for Percy then started to inform him.

"You quote from the poem about Cynara,

" 'I have been faithful to thee, Cynara! in my fashion.'

"You then comment, 'Yes, that was always Dowson's way, even to the point of dying in the arm of another man's wife—his best friend's!'—That's what you wrote, is it not?"

"It must be," said Guy, sinking into his chair, "if you say so."

"And yet you know as well as I do," shouted Percy, "that Sherrard rescued Dowson from a pub and took him home to be nursed and fed. And Dowson did indeed die in Mrs. Sherrard's arms, you utter snake; she was sustaining and comforting him in a sudden last spasm of his consumption. You know that as well as I do. And yet you write as if Dowson and she—"

"I am but a hardened old critic," said Guy.

Percy banged his fist on the table. "Critic— You're an unutterable rat."

"A hardened old journalist," said Guy.

"A steaming scorpion. Where is your charity?"

"I know nothing of charity," said Guy. "I have never heard of the steaming properties of the scorpion. I never cared for Dowson's verse."

"You're a blackguard—you've slandered his person. This has nothing to do with verse."

"What I wrote is the sort of thing, in my opinion, that *might* have happened," said Guy. "It is as near enough my meaning."

"A cheap jibe," yelled Percy. "Anything for a cheap joke, you'd say anything—"

"It was quite cheap, I admit," said Guy. "I am underpaid for these essays of mine."

Percy grabbed one of Guy's sticks which were propped beside his chair. Guy grabbed the other stick and, calling out for Tony, looked up with his schoolboy face obliquely at Percy.

"You will write a retraction," said Percy Mannering, with his wolf-like look, "or I'll knock your mean little brains out."

Guy aimed weakly with his stick at Percy's stick, and almost succeeded in knocking it out of the old man's quivering hand. Percy adjusted his stick, got it in both hands and with it knocked Guy's stick to the floor, just as Tony came in with a tray and a rattle of glasses.

"Jesus, Mary," said Tony and put down the tray.

"Tony, will you kindly recover my walking stick from Mr. Mannering."

Percy Mannering stood fiercely displaying his two greenish teeth and gripping the stick ready to strike, it seemed, anyone.

Tony slithered cautiously round the room until Guy's desk was between him and Percy. He lowered his head, rolled up his eyes, and glared at them from beneath his sandy eyebrows like a bull about to charge, except that he did not really look like a bull. "Take care what ye do," he said to them both.

Percy removed one of his hands from the shaking stick and took up the offensive journal. He fluttered this at Tony.

"Your master," he declared, "has uttered a damnable lie about a dead friend of mine."

" 'Tis within the realm of possibility," said Tony, clutching the edge of the desk.

"If you will lay a piece of writing paper on the desk, Tony," said Guy, "Mr. Mannering wishes to write a letter of protest to the editor of the magazine which he holds in his hand."

The poet grinned wildly. The telephone, which was on a side table beside Guy's chair, mercifully rang out.

"Come and answer the phone," said Guy to Tony.

But Tony was looking at Percy Mannering who still clung to the stick.

The telephone rang on.

"If ye will lift the instrument I'll lay out the paper as requested," said Tony, "for a man can do but one thing at a time." He opened a drawer and extracted a sheet of paper.

"Oh, it's you," Guy was saying, "well now, sonny, I'm busy at the moment. I have a poet friend here with me and we are just about to have a drink."

Guy heard the clear boyish voice continue: "Is it Mr. Percy Mannering who's with you?"

"That's right," said Guy.

"I'd like to talk to him."

"For you," said Guy, offering the receiver to Percy.

"Me? Who wants me, what?"

"For you," said Guy, "a youngster of school age I should think."

Percy bawled suspiciously into the telephone, "Hallo, who's there?"

"Remember you must die," said a man's voice, not at all that of a young person.

"This is Mannering here. Percy Mannering."

"That's correct," said the voice, and rang off.

Percy looked round the room with a bewildered air. "That's the chap they're talking about," he said.

"Drinks, Tony," said Guy.

"That's the man," roared Percy, his eyes gleaming as with some inner greed.

"Nice youngster, really. I suppose he's been overworking at his exams. The cops will get him, of course."

"That wasn't a youngster," said Percy, lifting his drink and draining it off, "it was a strong mature voice, very noble, like W. B. Yeats."

"Fill Mr. Mannering's glass, Tony," said Guy. "Mr. Mannering will be staying for dinner."

Percy took his drink, laid down the stick, and sank into a chair.

"What an experience!" he said.

"Intimations of immortality," commented Guy.

Percy looked at Guy and pointed to the telephone. "Are you behind this?"

"No," said Guy.

"No." The old man drained his glass, looked at the clock and rose from his chair. "I'll miss my train," he said.

"Stop the night," said Guy. "Do stay."

Percy walked uncertainly about the room. He picked up the magazine, and said,

"Look here—"

"There is a sheet of paper laid out for you to write your protest to the editor," Guy said.

"Yes," said the old man. "I'll do that tomorrow."

"There is a passage in *Childe Harold,*" said Guy, "I would like to discuss with you. It—"

"No one," stated Percy, "in the past fifty years has understood *Childe Harold.* You have to *begin* with the last two cantos, man. That is the SECRET of the poem. The episodes—"

Tony put his head round the door. "Did ye call me?"

"No, but while you're here, Mr. Mannering will be stopping the night."

Percy stayed the night and wrote his letter of protest to the editor next morning. He stayed for three weeks during which time he wrote a Shakespearian sonnet entitled "Memento Mori," the final couplet of the first version being,

> Out of the deep resounds the hollow cry,
> *Remember—oh, remember you must die!*

The second version being,

> But slowly the reverberating sigh
> Sounds in my ear: *Remember you must die!*

The third being,

> And from afar the Voices mingle and cry
> O mortal Man, *remember you must die!*

and there were many other revisions and versions.

Eric Colston and Mrs. Pettigrew were waiting for Godfrey's return.

"There's something funny going on in the old man's mind to-day," Mrs. Pettigrew said. "I should judge it was something to do with a visit from old Warner this morning. He couldn't have stayed long. I had just gone across the road for cigarettes and when I got back there was Warner on the doorstep. I asked him if he wanted to see Godfrey. He said, 'I've seen Godfrey, thanks.' But I'll find out what it's all about—you just wait, I'll find out. Then, when I got indoors Godfrey gave me a really wild grin and then *he* went out. I was too late to catch him. He didn't come back to lunch, there's his fish fingers lying on the table. Oh, I'll find out."

"Has he signed the will yet?" said Eric.

"No, the lawyers are taking their time."

Eric thought: I'll bet they are taking their time. He had taken the first train to London on receiving that letter from Olive. His first action had been to call on the solicitor. His next was to get in touch with Mrs. Pettigrew.

Mrs. Pettigrew filled Eric's glass. She noticed, as she had done earlier in the day, his little hands, and she felt quite frightened.

Eric was a stocky man, rather resembling his mother in appearance except that the feminine features and build looked odd in him. His hips were broad, his head was large. He had Charmian's wide-spaced eyes, pointed chin and small neat nose. His mouth was large like that of Dame Lettie whose battered body was later that evening to be discovered.

But, Mrs. Pettigrew told herself, she was experienced with men like Eric. Not that she had ever encountered quite the same details of behaviour in any other man. But she was familiar with the general pattern; she knew he was not normal, for though he greatly desired money he yet seemed willing to sacrifice quantities of it to gain some more intense and sinuous satisfaction. She had in her life before met men prepared to sacrifice the prospect of money in order to gain, for instance, a social ambition.

To that extent she felt she knew her man. She felt it

was not surprising that such a man would sacrifice anything for revenge. And yet, could she trust him?

"I am doing this," he had told her, "for moral reasons. I believe—I firmly believe, it will do the old man good. Teach him a lesson."

Oh, but Eric was a mess! She looked at his little hands and the feminine setting of the eyes like Charmian's and felt perhaps she was foolish to trust him.

Eric was a mess. Olive's letter had told him his father was being blackmailed by "a certain Mrs. Pettigrew" into bequeathing a large portion of his fortune to her. Eric had acted promptly and without a moment's thought. Even in the train up from Cornwall he had not taken thought but had flirted all the way with delicious ideas—the discomfiture of Godfrey; the undermining of Charmian; the possible sympathetic-bosomed qualities of this Mrs. Pettigrew under her possibly tough exterior; the thrill of being able to expose everyone to everyone if it proved expedient to do so; and the thrill of obtaining sufficient immediate cash to enable him to go and tell his Aunt Lettie what he really thought of her.

Not that he knew what he thought of her. He retained in his mind an axiom from his youth: the family had let him down badly. Everyone, even the family, had agreed upon that in the years when Eric was between twenty-two and twenty-eight, and the century was between twenty-three and twenty-nine years old. He had rejected every idea his family had ever held except this one idea, "Somehow or other we have let Eric down. How did it happen? Poor Eric, Charmian has mothered him too much. Charmian has not been a mother enough to him. Godfrey has been too occupied, has never taken any notice of the boy. Godfrey has been too lenient, too strict, too mean, has given him too much money." The elders had grown out of these sayings when the fashion changed, but by then

Eric had taken them for his creed. Lettie bore him off on consoling holidays. He robbed her, and the hotel staff got the blame. She tried to get him interested in prison-visiting. He started smuggling letters and tobacco into Wormwood Scrubs. "Poor Eric, he hasn't had a chance. He should never have been sent to that crank school. How could he ever be expected to pass an exam? I blame Charmian . . . I blame Lettie . . . Godfrey has never cared . . ." He went to an art school and was caught stealing six tubes of paint. They sent him to a Freudian analyst whom he did not like. They sent him to an Adlerian, and subsequently to an individualist. Meanwhile, there was an incident with a junior porter of a club, in the light of which he was sent to another psychiatrist of sympathetic persuasion. He was so far cured that he got one of the maids into trouble. Charmian was received into the Church.

"Eric will grow out of this phase," said Charmian. "My grandfather was wild as a youth."

But Eric was amazed when his elders eventually stopped blaming themselves for his condition. He thought them hypocritical and callous to go back on their words. He longed for them to start discussing him again in the old vein; but by the time he was thirty-seven they had said quite bitter things to him. He had bought a cottage in Cornwall, where he drank their money. He was in a home for inebriates when the war broke out. He emerged to be called up by the military, but was turned down on account of his psychological history. He loathed Charmian, Godfrey and Lettie. He loathed his cousin Martin who was doing so well as an engineer and who, as a child, had always been considered dull in comparison with Eric. He married a negress and got divorced six months later; a settlement being made on her by Godfrey. From time to time he wrote to Charmian, Godfrey and Lettie, to tell them that he loathed them. When, in 1947, Godfrey refused him any more money, he made it up with Lettie and obtained small revenues and larger promises from her. But Lettie, when she saw so little return for her cash by way of his company, reduced her bounty to mere talk about her will. Eric wrote a novel, and got it published on the strength of Charmian's name. It bore a similarity to Charmian's writing. "Poor Eric," said Charmian, "has not much originality. But I do think, Godfrey, now that he is really doing some work, we ought to assist him." She sent him, over a period of two years, all she possessed. Eric thought her mean, he thought her envious of his novel, and said so. Godfrey refused to write him. Charmian had confided to Guy Leet, "I suspect that Godfrey has a secret horror of another novelist in the family." And she added, what was not strictly true, but was a neat conclusion, "Of course, Godfrey always wanted Eric to join that dreary firm."

By the time he was fifty Eric began to display what looked like a mind of his own. That is, instead of sending wild vituperative accusations to his family, he now sent cold reasoned denunciations. He proved, point by point, that they had let him down badly from the time of his first opening his eyes.

"In his middle-age Eric is becoming so like Godfrey," said Charmian, "though of course, Godfrey does not see it."

Eric no longer called Charmian's novels lousy muck. He analysed them piece by piece, he ridiculed the spare parts, he demolished the lot. He had some friends who applauded his efforts.

"But he takes my work so seriously," said Charmian. "Nobody ever wrote of it like that."

Charmian's health had failed by the mid-fifties. The revival of her novels astonished Eric, for he had by some fractional oversight misjudged an element in the temper of his age. He canvassed his friends and was angered and bewildered to find so many had fallen for the Charmian Piper period-cult.

Charmian's remittances, smuggled through Mrs. Anthony, were received with silence. His second book had secretly appealed to Dame Lettie. It had been described as "realistic and brutally frank," but the energy which he might have put into developing his realistic and brutally frank talents was now dispersed in resentment against Charmian. The revival of her novels finished him off and he found he could no longer write.

Even the reports in the papers that Godfrey, Charmian and Lettie had been recipients of threatening telephone calls failed to stimulate him.

Throughout the war, and since, he had been mainly living on women of means, the chief of whom had been Lisa Brooke. He had found it hard, after Lisa's death, to replace her. Everyone was hard up, and Eric put on weight with the worry of it all, which did not help. His difficulties were approaching a climax at the moment he had received Olive's letter. "Your father is being cruelly blackmailed by a certain Mrs. Pettigrew, the housekeeper. I think he would be willing to make up the past differences, if there was anything you could do without letting your mother know. . . ."

He took the first train up to London, in a state of excitement, and spent the journey visualising the possibilities before him.

When he arrived at Paddington at a quarter to six he had no idea what he was going to do. He went into the bar and had a drink. At seven he emerged and saw a telephone box. He telephoned to the home of his father's solicitor, and on the strength of his communication, obtained an interview that evening. He got from the solicitor an assurance that preparations for the new will would be delayed as long as possible. He received some additional advice to which he did not listen.

He went to call on Olive, but found her flat deserted. He stayed the night with some reluctant acquaintances in Notting Hill Gate. At eleven next morning he telephoned to Mrs. Pettigrew and met her for lunch in a café in Kensington.

"I wish you to know, Mrs. Pettigrew," he said, "that I'm with you. The old man deserves a lesson. I take the moral point of view, and I'm quite willing to forgo the money."

"I'm sure," said Mrs. Pettigrew at first, "I don't know what you mean, Mr. Eric." She wiped the corners of her mouth with her handkerchief, pulling her lower lip askew in the process.

"He would die," said Eric, "rather than my poor mother got to know about his gross infidelities. And so would I. In fact, Mrs. Pettigrew," he said with his smile which had long ceased to be winning, "you have us both in your hands, my father and I."

Mrs. Pettigrew said, "I've done a lot for your parents. Your poor mother, before she was taken away, I had to do *everything* for her. There aren't many that would have put up with so much. Your mother was inclined to be— well, you know what old people are. I suppose I'm old myself, but—"

"Not a bit," said Eric. "You don't look a day older than sixty."

"Well, I felt my years while I had your mother to attend to."

"I'm sure you did. She's impossibly conceited," said Eric; "impossible."

"Quite impossible. And, now, your father—"

"He's impossible," said Eric, "an old brute."

"What exactly," said Mrs. Pettigrew, "had you in mind, Mr. Eric?"

"Well, I felt it my duty to stand behind you. And here I am. Money," he said, "means hardly anything to me."

"Ah, you can't go far without money, Mr. Eric—"

"Do call me Eric," he said.

"Eric," she said, "your best friend's your—"

"Well, of course, a little cash at the right time is always useful. At the right time. It's surprising, really, my father has lived so long after the life he's led."

"Eric, I would never let you go short. I mean, until the time comes . . ."

"You can always get ready cash out of him?"

"Oh yes."

Eric thought: I bet you can.

"I think we should see him together," said Eric.

She looked at his little hands. Can I trust him? she wondered. The will was not yet signed and sealed.

"Trust me," said Eric. "Two heads are better than one."

"I would like to think it over," she said.

"You would prefer to work alone?"

"Oh, don't say that. I mean, this plan of yours is rather sudden, and I feel, after all I've done for Godfrey and Charmian, I'm entitled to—"

"Perhaps, after all," said Eric, "it is my duty to go down to Surrey to see Mother and inform her of her husband's little indiscretions. Distasteful as that course might be, in fact, it might save a lot of trouble. It would take a load off my father's mind, and there would then be no need for you to take any further interest in him. It must be a strain on you."

She came back on him sharply: "You don't know the details of your father's affairs. I do. You have no evidence. I have. Written proof."

"Oh yes," he said, "I have evidence."

Is it bluff? she wondered.

"When do you want to come and see him?" she said.

"Now," he said.

But when they got back, Godfrey was still out. Mrs.

Anthony had left. Mrs. Pettigrew felt quite frightened. And when Eric started roaming about the house, picking up the china ornaments and turning them upside down to look at them, she felt quite vexed. But she held her peace. She felt she knew her man. At least she ought to, with all her experience.

When he sat down, eventually, in Charmian's old chair, she ruffled his hair, and said, "Poor Eric. You've had a raw deal from them, haven't you?" He leaned his large head against her bosom and felt quite nice.

After tea Mrs. Pettigrew had a slight attack of asthma and withdrew to the garden, where she got it under control. On her return she thought she saw Godfrey in the chair where she had left Eric. But it was Eric all right. He was asleep, his head lolling sideways; although in features he most resembled Charmian, he looked remarkably like Godfrey in this pose.

Charmian's impression of Godfrey's brightness and health, when she saw him from her window, became more pronounced when he was shown into her room.

"Cheerful place," he said, looking round.

"Come and sit down, Godfrey. Guy Leet had just gone. I'm afraid I'm rather tired."

"Yes, I saw him leaving."

"Yes, poor soul. It was kind of him to visit me. He has such difficulty getting about."

"So different," said Godfrey, leaning back in his chair like a satisfied man, and stretching his legs apart, "from the way he got about in the summer of 1902 in the villa on Lake Geneva, up to 1907 at his flat in Hyde Park Gate, in Scotland and Biarritz and Torquay and then in the Dolomites when you were taken ill. Then nineteen years later when he was living in Ebury Street, up to the time of—"

"I should like a cigarette," said Charmian.

"What?" said Godfrey.

"Give me a cigarette, Godfrey, or I shall ring and ask the nurse to fetch one."

"Look here, Charmian, you'd better stay off cigarettes. I mean—"

"I would like to smoke a cigarette before I die. As to Guy Leet—you yourself, Godfrey, have hardly any room to talk. You yourself. Lisa Brooke. Wendy Loos. Eleanor—"

"The little rotter," said Godfrey. "Well, just look what he's come to and only seventy-five. Bent double over two sticks."

"Jean Taylor must have talked," she said. She stretched out her hand and said, "A cigarette, Godfrey." He gave her one and lit it.

"I'm getting rid of Mrs. Pettigrew," he said. "A most domineering bitch. Always upsetting Mrs. Anthony."

Charmian inhaled her cigarette. "Any other news?" she said.

"Alec Warner," he said, "is losing control of his faculties. He came to see me this morning and wanted me to take my pulse and temperature. I ordered him out of the house."

Charmian began to laugh, and could not stop, and eventually had to be put to bed, while Godfrey was taken away and given a soft-boiled egg with thin bread and butter, and sent off home.

At eight o'clock they had finished supper. Mrs. Pettigrew said, "If he isn't home by nine I'd better ring the police. He might have had an accident. That car, it isn't safe. He's a menace on the road."

"I shouldn't worry," said Eric, reflecting that, after all, the new will was not signed.

"Oh, I always worry about him," she said. "That's what I mean when I say that I'm entitled to . . ."

Godfrey drove more carefully than usual. Having satisfied himself that Warner's information was accurate he
felt that life was worth taking care of. Not that one had
doubted Warner's information. Poor Charmian. At any
rate, she had no call, now, to be uppish and righteous.
Not that she really had been priggish; but she had always
assumed that air of purity which made one feel such a
swine. Poor Charmian; it was very catty of Taylor to
gossip about her after all these years. Still, Taylor had
done one a good turn without knowing it. . . .

Here he was at home. A long drive for an old man.

Godfrey came in with his glasses in his hand, rubbing
his eyes.

"Where on earth have you been?" said Mrs. Pettigrew.
"Eric is here to see you."

"Oh, good evening, Eric," said Godfrey. "Have a
drink."

"I've got one," said Eric.

"I'm keeping quite well, thank you," said Godfrey,
raising his voice.

"Oh, really?" said Eric.

"Eric wishes to speak to you Godfrey."

"Mrs. Pettigrew and I are in this together, Father."

"In what?"

"The question of the new will. And in the meantime,
I expect to be remunerated according to the situation."

"You're growing a paunch," said Godfrey. "I haven't
got a paunch."

"Otherwise we shall really have to present Mother with
the facts."

"Be reasonable, Godfrey," said Mrs. Pettigrew.

"Get to hell out of my house, Eric," said Godfrey. "I
give you ten minutes or I call the police."

"I think we're a little tired," said Mrs. Pettigrew, "aren't
we?"

"And you leave tomorrow morning," he said to her.

The door bell rang.

"Who can that be?" said Mrs. Pettigrew. "Did you forget to leave the car lights on, Godfrey?"

Godfrey ignored the bell. "You can't tell Charmian anything," he said, "that she doesn't know already."

"What did you say?" said Mrs. Pettigrew.

The door bell rang again.

Godfrey left them and went to open it. Two men stood on the doorstep.

"Mr. Colston?"

"That's right."

"Could we have word with you? It's the C.I.D."

"The car lights are on," said Godfrey.

"It's about your sister," said the senior-looking of the men, "Dame Lettie Colston, I'm afraid."

Next day was Sunday. "HOAX CALLER STRIKES AT LAST" declared the headlines. *"Aged Welfare Worker, 81, killed in bed. Jewellery and valuables missing."*

Chapter Fifteen

"If you look for one thing," said Henry Mortimer to his wife, "you frequently find another."

Mrs. Mortimer was opening and closing her mouth like a bird. This was because she was attempting to feed a two-year-old boy with a spoon, and as he opened his mouth to take each spoonful of soft egg, she involuntarily opened hers. This child was her grandson whom she was minding while her daughter was confined with a second child.

Mrs. Mortimer wiped the infant's mouth and pushed a jug of milk out of his reach.

"Look for one thing and you find another," said Henry Mortimer. "They found twenty-two different wills amongst Lettie Colston's papers, dated over the past forty years."

"Silly woman," said Emmeline Mortimer, "to change her mind so often." She tickled the cheek of her grandson and clucked into his face, and while his mouth was open in laughter she popped in the last spoonful of egg, most of which he spluttered out. "I was sorry for poor old Godfrey breaking down at the inquest. He must have been fond of his sister," she said.

She gave the child his mug of milk which he clutched in both hands and drank noisily, his eyes bright above the rim, darting here and there.

When the child was settled in a play-pen in the garden Mrs. Mortimer said to her husband,

"What's that you were saying about poor Lettie Colston's wills?"

"The chaps were checking up on her papers in the course of routine, in case they should provide any clue to the murder, and of course they checked up on all her beneficiaries. Quite a list out of twenty-two consecutive wills."

"The murderer wasn't known to her, was he?"

"No—oh no, this was before they got him. They were checking up, and . . ."

Dame Lettie's murderer had been caught within three weeks of her death and was now awaiting trial. In those three weeks, however, her papers had been thoroughly examined, and those of the beneficiaries of her twenty-two wills who were still alive had been quietly traced, checked, and dismissed from suspicion. Only one name had proved a very slight puzzle; Lisa O'Brien of Nottingham, whose name appeared in a bequest dated 1918. The records, however, showed that Lisa Brooke, nee Sidebottome, aged 33, had married a man named Matthew O'Brien aged 40 at Nottingham in that year. The C.I.D. did not look much further. Lisa O'Brien in the will must be a woman of advanced years by now and, in fact, it emerged that she was dead; O'Brien himself, if still alive, would be beyond the age of the suspect. The police were no longer interested, and ticked the name O'Brien off their list.

Henry Mortimer, however, as one acquainted with the murdered woman and her circle, had been approached, and had undertaken to investigate any possible connection between the murder and the anonymous telephone calls. Not that the police believed these calls had taken place; every possible means of detection had failed, and they had concluded, with the support of their psychologists, that the old people were suffering from hallucinations.

The public, however, had to be satisfied. Henry Mortimer was placed in charge of this side of the case. The police were able to announce:

The possibility of a connection between the murder and the anonymous telephone calls which the murdered woman was reported to receive from time to time before her death, is being investigated.

Mortimer fulfilled his duties carefully. Like his colleagues, he suspected the murderer to be a chance criminal. Like his colleagues, he knew the anonymous voice would never be traced in flesh and blood. Nevertheless, he examined the police documents, and finally sent in a report which enabled the police to issue a further statement:

The authorities are satisfied that there is no connection between the murder of Dame Lettie Colston and the anonymous telephone calls of which she had been complaining some months before her death.

Meantime, however, Henry had noticed the details of Lisa O'Brien, and was interested.

"You look for one thing and you find another," he had said to himself. For he had never before heard of this marriage of Lisa's. Her first marriage with rich old Brooke had been dissolved in 1912. Her secret marriage with Guy Leet had recently come to light, when Guy had claimed her fortune. But Matthew O'Brien—Henry did not recall any Matthew O'Brien. He must be quite old now, probably dead.

He had requested the C.I.D. to check further on Matthew O'Brien. And they had found him quite quickly, in a mental home in Folkestone where he had been resident for more than forty years.

"And so," said Mortimer to his wife, "you look for one thing and you find another."

"Do Janet and Ronald Sidebottome know anything of this husband?" said Mrs. Mortimer.

"Yes, they remember him quite well. Lisa went touring Canada with him. They didn't hear from her for a year. When she turned up again she told them he had been killed in an accident."

"How long has he been in this mental home?"

"Since 1919—a few months after their marriage. Janet is going down to identify him tomorrow."

"That will be difficult after all these years."

"It is only a formality. The man is undoubtedly Matthew O'Brien whom Lisa Brooke married in 1918."

"And she said he was dead?"

"Yes, she did."

"Well, what about Guy Leet? Didn't she marry him? That make them bigamists, doesn't it?"

"I shouldn't think for a moment Guy knew the man was still alive. Everyone, apparently believed he was dead."

"The police won't trouble poor Guy about it?"

"Oh, the police won't bother him now. Especially at his age."

"What a woman," said Mrs. Mortimer, "that Lisa Brooke was. Well, I expect her money—Oh, what will happen to her money, now? Guy Leet is surely—"

"That's a question, indeed. Lisa's fortune belongs to Matthew O'Brien by rights, sane or insane."

Henry went out into the garden and said to his squealing grandson,

"What's all this racket going on?" He rolled him over and over on the warm stubbly grass. He picked up the child and threw him into the blue sky and caught him again.

"He'll throw up his breakfast," remarked Emmeline, who stood with her head on one side, and smiled proudly at the child.

"Up-up-ee," demanded the child.

Henry rolled him over and over, left him yelling for more, and went indoors to catch Alec Warner on the telephone before he should go out.

"You're interested in the St. Aubrey's Home at Folkestone?" Henry said.

"Yes. But only in the older patients. I've been visiting them on private research for ten years."

"Do you know a man there called Matthew O'Brien?"

"Matt O'Brien, oh yes, a private patient. A dear old chap, nearly eighty. He's bedridden now. Quite batty, of course, but he always knows me."

"Were you thinking," said Henry, "of going down there any time this week?"

"Well, I only go once a month, as a rule, and I went last week. Is there anything special?"

"Only," said Henry, "that Janet Sidebottome has agreed to go down to Folkestone tomorrow to identify Matthew O'Brien. I won't go into details, but if you would care to accompany her, since you are acquainted with the home, it would be a kindness to Janet who will probably be distressed. Ronald can't go with her, he's in bed with a chill."

"What has Janet Sidebottome to do with Matt O'Brien?"

"Can you go?" said Henry.

"Yes," said Alec.

"Then Janet will explain everything. Do you know her number?"

"Yes," said Alec.

"And one of our men will be there to meet you."

"A copper?" said Alec.

"A detective," said Mortimer. "The affair might be of some incidental interest to you."

"That's just what I was thinking," said Alec.

Janet said, "It is all most distressing. Ronald should have been here to assist me. He met Matthew several times. It can't think why Ronald should have a chill in this fine weather."

Alec shouted above the rattle of the taxi.

"No need to be distressed. I shall do my best to replace Ronald."

"Oh, no, don't distress Ronald," she said. "I only meant—"

He gave her a smile. She sadly adjusted her hearing equipment, and said, "My hearing is rather poor."

"You may not be able to recognise Matt O'Brien," he articulated. "He's an old man, and the years of insanity may have changed him beyond recognition. They get drugs, you know, and then the drugs have an affect on the appearance. But don't worry if his features are not familiar to you. I think the authorities already have evidence that he's Lisa's husband. They have Lisa's signature, for instance, from the time of his admission."

"I will do my best," said Janet. "But it is a distressing experience."

"He is gentle," shouted Alec. "He thinks he is God. He has never been violent."

"I am distressed about my late sister," Janet said. "I don't like to admit it, but I must; Lisa was never straight in her dealings. It is a blessing she was never found out in this business."

"It would have been bigamy," said Alec.

"It was bigamy," she said. "There was no excuse for Lisa, she had every opportunity in life. But it was the same when she was a girl. She caused our dear father a great deal of sorrow. And when Simon Brooke divorced her, there was all that scandal. Scandal was serious in those days."

"What did you think of Matt O'Brien at the time?"

"Well, he was an Irishman, a lawyer. He talked a great deal, but then he was an Irishman, and he was quite charming. And do you know, when Lisa told me he was dead, I could hardly believe it. He had seemed to me so lively. Of course, we did not suspect the truth. It is very distressing."

"It will soon be over," said Alec. "We shall not be with him for long."

The interview with Matt O'Brien was soon over. The detective met them in the hall and a nurse took them up to Matt's room where he lay on his pillow among his loose white hair.

"Hallo, Matt," said Alec, "I've brought two friends of mine to see you."

The detective nodded to the old man and stood back discreetly and formally beside the nurse.

Janet approached his bedside and lifted his limp hand in greeting. He raised his other hand in benediction.

The old man moved his pale eyes towards Alec.

"It's you, Alec," he said in a blurred voice, as if his tongue were in the way.

"I was wondering," said Alec, "if you remember a lady called Lisa, at all? Lisa Brooke. Lisa Sidebottome."

"Lisa," said the old man.

"You don't remember Lisa—a red-haired lady?" said Alec.

"Lisa," said the old man, looking at Janet.

"No, this isn't Lisa. This is her sister, Janet. She's come to see you."

The old man was still looking at Janet.

"Don't you remember Lisa?—Well, never mind," said Alec.

The old man shook his head. "I recollect all creatures," he said.

"Lisa died last year," Alec said. "I just thought you might know of her."

"Lisa," said the old man and looked out at the sky through the window. It was a bright afternoon, but he must have seen a night sky full of stars. "My stars are shining in the sky," he said. "Have I taken her to Myself?"

Janet was served with tea downstairs and invited to put her feet up for a while.

She put away her handkerchief. "I did not," she said, "at first find any resemblance. I thought there must be a mistake. But as he turned his head aside to the window, I saw the profile, I recognised his features quite plainly. Yes, I am sure he is the same Matthew O'Brien. And his manner, too, when he spoke of the stars. . . ."

Alec declined tea. He took a notebook from his pocket and tore a page from it.

"Will you excuse me if I scribble a note to a friend? I have to catch the post." He was already scribbling away when Miss Sidebottome gave him leave to do so.

> DEAR GUY—I believe I shall be the first to give you the following information.
>
> A man named Matthew O'Brien has been discovered, who was already married to Lisa when you married her.
>
> Mortimer will give you the details, which have now been fully established.
>
> As it happened, I have been visiting this man, in the course of research, at St. Aubrey's Home for mental cases, for the past ten years, without suspecting any such association.
>
> I imagine there will be no blame imputed to you. But of course, as your marriage with Lisa was invalid, you will not now benefit from her estate. Lisa's money, or at least the great bulk of it, will of course go to her legal husband—I fancy it will be kept in trust for him as he is mentally incapacitated.
>
> Be a good fellow, and, immediately on reading this letter, take your pulse and temperature, and let me know . . .

Alec begged an envelope from the receptionist. He slipped in his note, and addressed and stamped it. He slid the letter into the post-box in the hall, and returned to comfort Janet.

Alec felt, when he left Janet Sidebottome's hotel after escorting her painfully home, that he had had a fruitful though exhausting day.

Reflecting on Matt O'Brien's frail and sexless flesh and hair on his pillow, and how the old man had looked back and forth between Janet and himself, he was reminded of that near-centenarian, Mrs. Bean, who had replaced Granny Green in the Maud Long Ward. So different from each other in features, they yet shared this quality, that one would not know what was their sex from first impressions. He resolved to make a note of this in Matt O'Brien's case-history.

He felt suddenly tired and stopped a taxi. As it drove him home he ruminated on the question, why scientific observation differed from humane observation, and how the same people observed in these respective senses, actually seemed to be different people. He had to admit that Mrs. Bean, for instance, to whom he had not paid close attention, had none the less rewarded him with one of those small points of observation that frequently escaped him when he was deliberately watching his object. However, the method he had evolved was, on the whole, satisfactory.

A fire-engine clanged past. Alec leaned in his corner and closed his eyes. The taxi turned a corner. Alec shifted his position and looked out into the evening. The taxi was purring along the Mall towards St. James's Street.

The driver leaned back and opened the communicating window.

"A fire somewhere round here," he said.

Alec found himself on the pavement outside his block of chambers, in a crowd. There were policemen everywhere, smoke, people, firemen, water, then suddenly, a cry from the crowd and everyone looking up as a burst of flame shot from the top of the building.

Alec pushed through to the inner edge of the crowd. A policeman barred his way with a strong casual arm. "I live here," Alec explained. "Let me pass, please."

"Can't go in there," said the policeman. "Stand back, please."

"Get back," shouted the crowd.

Alec said, "But I live there. My things. Where's the porter?"

"The building is on fire, sir," said the policeman.

Alec made a rush advance and got past the policeman into the smoke and water at the entrance to the building. Someone hit him on the face. The crowd fell back as a wave of smoke and flame issued from a lower window. Alec stood and looked into the interior while another policeman from the opposite side of the crowd walked over to him.

"Come back," said the policeman, "you're obstructing the firemen."

"My papers are up there," Alec said.

The policeman took him by the arm and pulled him away. "There is a cat," Alec said desperately, "in my rooms. I can't let pussy burn. Let me dash up and let her out. I'll take the risk."

The policeman did not reply, but continued to propel Alec away from the fire.

"There's a dog up there. A beautiful husky from a polar expedition," Alec haggled. "Top floor, first door."

"Sorry, too late guvnor," said one of the firemen. "Your dog must have had it by now. The top storey's burnt out."

One of the residents among the crowd said, "There are no pets in those flats. Pets are not allowed."

Alec walked away, he went to his club and booked a room for the night.

Chapter Sixteen

The summer had passed and it was Granny Bean's birthday, for which the ward had been preparing for some days.

There was a huge cake with a hundred candles. Some men from the newspapers came in with their cameras. Others talked a while to Granny Bean, who was propped up in a new blue bed-jacket.

"Yes," Granny Bean answered them in her far-away flute, "I've lived a long time."

"Yes," said Granny Bean, "I'm very happy."

"That's right," she agreed, "I seen Queen Victoria once as a girl."

"What does it feel like to be a hundred, Mrs. Bean?"

"All right," she said weakly, nodding her head.

"You mustn't tire her," Sister Lucy who had put on her service medal for the occasion, told the newsmen.

The men took down notes from the sister. "Seven children, only one now alive, in Canada. Started life as a seamstress hand at the age of eleven. . . ."

The matron came in at three o'clock and read out the telegram from the Queen. Everyone applauded. Granny Valvona commented, "'. . . on your hundredth birthday,' doesn't sound quite right. Queen Mary always used to say, 'on the occasion of your centenary.'" But everyone said it came to the same thing.

The matron stood proxy for Granny Bean in blowing

out the candles. She was out of breath by the twenty-third. The nurses took turns to blow out the rest.

They were cutting the cake. One of the newsmen called, "Three cheers for Granny Bean."

The hilarity was dying down and the men had gone by the time the normal visitors started to arrive. Some of the geriatrics were still eating or doing various things with their slice of cake.

Miss Valvona adjusted her glasses and reached for the newspaper. She read out for the third time that day: " 'September 21st—to-day's birthday. Your year ahead: You can expect an eventful year. Controversial matters may predominate from December to March. People associated with music, transport, and the fashion industry will find the coming year will bring a marked progress.' Now, were you not connected with the fashion industry, Granny Bean? It says here in black and white . . ."

But Mrs. Bean had dropped asleep on her pillow after the nurse had given her a warm drink. Her mouth was formed once more into a small "O" through which her breath whistled faintly.

"Festivities going on?" said Alec Warner, looking around at the party decorations.

"Yes, Mrs. Bean is a hundred to-day."

The deep lines on Alec's face and brow showed deeper. It was four months since he had lost his entire notes and records in the fire.

Jean Taylor had said, "Try to start all over again, Alec. You will find a lot of it will come back to your mind while you work."

"I could never trust my memory," he had said, "as I trusted those notes."

"Well, you must start all over again."

"I haven't got it in me," he said, "to do that at my age. It was an accumulation of years of labour. It was invaluable."

He had seldom, since then, referred to his loss. He felt, sometimes, he said once, that he was really dead, since his records had ceased to exist.

"That's rather a metaphysical idea for you, Alec," she said. "For in fact you are not dead, but still alive."

He told her, it was true he frequently went over his vast notebooks in his mind, as through a card index. "But never," he said, "shall I make another note. I read instead. It is in some ways a better thing."

She caught him looking almost desirously at Granny Bean on her hundredth birthday. He sighed and looked away.

"We all appear to ourselves frustrated in our old age, Alec, because we cling to everything so much. But in reality we are still fulfilling our lives."

"A friend of mine fulfilled his yesterday."

"Oh, who was that?"

"Matt O'Brien in Folkestone. He thought he was God. He died in his sleep. He has left a fortune, but never knew about it. Lisa's money of course. No relatives."

"Will Guy Leet—?"

"No, Guy has no claim. I think Lisa's estate will now go according to her will to Mrs. Pettigrew."

"In that case," said Miss Taylor, "she will, after all, have her reward."

Mrs. Pettigrew had her reward. Lisa's will was proved in her favour and she inherited all her fortune. After her first stroke Mrs. Pettigrew went to live in a hotel at South Kensington. She is still to be seen at eleven in the morning at Harrod's Bank where she regularly meets some of the other elderly residents to discuss the shortcomings of the hotel management, and to plan various campaigns against the staff. She can still be seen in the evening jostling for a place by the door of the hotel lounge before the dinner gong sounds.

Charmian died one morning in the following spring, at the age of eighty-seven.

Godfrey died the same year as the result of a motor accident, his car having collided with another at a bend in Kensington Church Street. He was not killed outright, but died a few days later of pneumonia which had set in from the shock. It was the couple in the other car who were killed outright.

Guy Leet died at the age of seventy-eight.

Percy Mannering is in an old men's home, where he is known as "The Professor" and is treated with special respect, having his bed put in an alcove at the far corner of the dormitory—a position reserved for patients who have known better days. His grand-daughter, Olive, sometimes visits him. She takes away his poems and letters to editors; she types them out, and despatches them according to Percy's directions.

Ronald Sidebottome is allowed up in the afternoons but is not expected to last another winter.

Janet Sidebottome died of a stroke following an increase in blood pressure, at the age of seventy-seven.

Mrs. Anthony, now widowed, had a legacy from Charmian, and has gone to live at a seaside town, near her married son. Sometimes, when she hears of old people receiving anonymous telephone calls, she declares it is a good thing, judging by what she has seen, that she herself is hard of hearing.

Chief Inspector Mortimer died suddenly of heart-failure at the age of seventy-three, while boarding his yacht, *The Dragonfly*. Mrs. Mortimer spends most of her time looking after her numerous grandchildren.

Eric is getting through the Colston money which came to him on the death of his father.

Alec Warner had a paralytic stroke following a cerebral haemorrhage. For a time he was paralysed on one side and his speech was incoherent. In time he regained the use of his limbs, his speech improved. He went to live permanently in a nursing home and frequently searched through his mind, as through a card index, for the case-histories of his friends, both dead and dying.

What were they sick, what did they die of?

Lettie Colston, he recited to himself, comminuted fractures of the skull; Godfrey Colston, hypostatic pneumonia; Charmian Colston, uraemia; Jean Taylor, myocardial degeneration; Tempest Sidebottome, carcinoma of the cervix; Ronald Sidebottome, carcinoma of the bronchus; Guy Leet, arterio-sclerosis; Henry Mortimer, coronary thrombosis. . . .

Miss Valvona went to her rest. Many of the grannies followed her. Jean Taylor lingered for a time, employing her pain to magnify the Lord, and meditating sometimes confidingly upon Death, the first of the Four Last Things to be ever remembered.